ABOUT THE AUTHOR

Joan Lingard has published more than thirty books for children and thirteen for adults. *Tug of War* was shortlisted for the Carnegie Medal, the Federation of Children's Book Groups Award, the Lancashire Children's Book Club of the Year, and the Sheffield Book Award. *The Guilty Party* was also shortlisted for the Federation of Children's Book Groups Award. Joan was awarded the M.B.E. in 1998. She is married with three children and four grandchildren.

'I was born in Edinburgh but grew up in Belfast where I lived until the age of eighteen. I was an avid reader when I was young (still am!) and could never get enough to read. I used to go to my local children's library, a poor affair housed in something resembling a shed, and no bigger. The books were all ancient and had lost their dust wrappers, and the pages were often spattered with the remains of other readers' meals, but it would have taken more than that to put me off. I read very fast and when I finished a book I moaned in my mother's ear about having nothing to read. One day, fed up with me, she said, "Why don't you write a book of your own?" 'Why not?' I thought. I took lined, foolscap paper, filled my fountain pen with green ink (I thought that would be artistic!), and I began to write my very first novel. From that moment on I wanted to be a novelist, and nothing else.'

Joan Lingard

A Secret Place

Joan Lingard

Hodder
Children's
Books

a division of Hodder Headline plc

For Shona and Amy
and Rosa
with love

One

It was on the first of March, our father's birthday, that we were snatched from the school playground. At the time we didn't know he was 'snatching' us. We thought he'd just turned up to take us out. Or that was what *I* thought. My brother Carlos, more commonly known as Charlie, is only six, five years my junior, and so he's a bit on the young side to think very much, at least about things like *that*.

My father had picked a good day to come. I'd had a row with my mother that morning. We'd slept in and she was annoyed about that to start with. She'd got me up in the end by slinging a wet cloth across my face. I shot upright, spluttering. I told her she was a brute. She says I exaggerate but it seems to me that wakening someone like that could only be called brutal.

'You know I've got to get going early this morning!' she said.

I'd forgotten. I'd been having a nice sleepy dream, the kind you have when you're half awake and half asleep. I'd been dreaming that I was with my father in Andalucia, in the south of Spain, walking over the high sierras with a wide blue sky spanning us overhead, stretching wide in every direction. Beyond, I'd seen a scribble of marine blue that marked the

Mediterranean shore. And behind us a brilliant white village clung to the hillside looking as if it might slip and slide at any moment. I didn't want the dream to end. I held on to it like mad even though my mother's voice was doing its best to shatter it. Did eventually shatter it. Afterwards, the dream seemed to have been a kind of prophecy.

I'd forgotten that my mother was going to Sheffield on business. I'm not sure exactly what she does but she's employed by an insurance company and she goes to work in a neat suit, either navy blue or dark grey. Today she was wearing the grey, with a red and white striped blouse. She never dressed like that when we lived in Spain. She says it's called 'power dressing'. It makes her feel more powerful when she has to negotiate with people at work. 'You mean you can boss them?' I asked her. She didn't answer that.

She was to be away for three days and Charlie and I were to go and stay with her sister, our Aunt Heather. Now I didn't want to go to Aunt Heather's. For one thing she moans and criticises from morning till night. No matter what you do she's never pleased. You could run messages for her till you were out of puff and wash all her dishes and she'd still make some crack about it being all right for someone with nothing else to do but lounge around all day!

The other thing was that I wanted to be with my best friend Shona at her house. I desperately wanted to. We were going to have a midnight feast, and on that night my other best friend Amy would come. I'd already bought a packet of chocolate biscuits and two cans of Coke that I'd stowed away under my bed.

2

'You are going to stay with Aunt Heather!' said my mother, shovelling muesli into my bowl. She *was* in a snappy mood this morning!

'I'm not hungry,' I said, staring at the mound of muesli.

Charlie was tucking into his cornflakes and reading the back of the packet.

'Why can't I stay with Shona?' I was not for giving up easily. I sometimes found if I ground on long enough I'd get on her nerves and she'd give in. 'Her mum asked me to stay. She'll be offended if I don't go. She'll think you think they're not good enough for us.'

'Don't be ridiculous!' My mother pulled up her tights – she was finishing her dressing in the kitchen where she could keep an eye on us – and yanked a big hole in one leg where it would show under the hem of her skirt. We kept our heads down until she'd stopped swearing and had gone in search of a new, unholey pair.

She came back wearing them and carrying a small suitcase. She was ready for the road but we were not.

'If you're not hungry then starve!' She tipped the muesli back into the jar just as I was beginning to feel hungry. 'Go to the loo now and wash your hands and faces and comb your hair. *Rapido*!'

She shouldn't have said '*Rapido*' for that made us think of our father, Antonio.

'Do you know what day it is, Mum?' cried Charlie. 'It's Papa's birthday!'

Charlie had circled the date in waxy red crayon on the wall calendar and we'd sent cards and presents. Not our mother, of course. I'd bought him a tartan tie and Charlie had made him a felt purse at school.

I had written on my card: 'Please come and see us soon. I am missing you very much.' I'd sealed the envelope before my mother saw what I'd written. She'd have been furious with me and would probably have torn up the card. We hadn't seen him since they had separated two years ago. No, maybe she wouldn't have gone quite *that* far. I was missing him terribly though I wasn't so sure that Charlie was. At times I thought he'd almost forgotten what our father was like. I kept a photograph of him on top of my dresser and Mum didn't dare take it down.

'Do you think he'll have a birthday party?' asked Charlie, in between having his face wiped by our mother. She'd brought the sponge to him in the end.

'I haven't the faintest idea!' she said, sponging him all the harder so that he tried to wriggle away, but she held on tight.

'I expect he will,' I said. 'With lots of singing and dancing.' I held my hands above my head and clicked my fingers and stamped my heels in a rapid tattoo. I imagined that I was a flamenco dancer with a fitting bodice and a red ruffled skirt. I had a dress like that upstairs but it had grown too tight for me. I reminded myself to write to Dad and ask him to send me a new one.

Our father is a flamenco dancer. That's how he earns his living. Some living! my mother would say. She hadn't seen a penny from him since the day they'd parted. I'd heard her say so more than once and wondered why she had to go on repeating herself.

4

I know I'm making my mum sound bitchy and rotten, but she's not like that all the time. She can be nice and soft and smiley when she wants to but not this morning when she was trying to get us off to school and herself on a train to Sheffield.

'Get your coats on!' she commanded.

I clicked my fingers again and said, '*Ole*!' which annoyed her. I had known it would. But she'd annoyed me by not agreeing to let me go and stay with Shona. I returned to the attack in the hope that she'd finally throw up her hands and say, 'All right then! All right, *go*!'

'Why *can't* I stay at Shona's? We could do our homework together.'

She didn't throw up her hands in surrender. She said, 'Oh yes, I can just imagine it! A fat lot of homework you would do! You are going to stay with your aunt whether you like it or not and I don't wish to hear one more word on the subject, Maria. Understand!'

'You're mean,' I told her.

'And you're a pain in the neck,' she told me.

I refused to kiss her goodbye and was to feel sorry about that later. I didn't even turn round to wave though Charlie did. He blew her kisses from his hand, walking backward. But how was I to know that our father would be waiting for us at the school gate at lunchtime?

Two

Charlie was so pleased to see our father that he jumped up into his arms like a monkey on a stick and shouted 'Happy Birthday, Papa!' Then he said, 'Are you going to have a party? Will we have ice cream? Can I have double chocolate chip?'

I couldn't believe it! There stood our father looking just as he had in my dream, his dark eyes sparkling with laughter and his face flushed. He throws his head back when he laughs. He is very handsome, Antonio, our father. Even our mother would admit that. Once upon a time they'd been in love with each other. She'd met him on holiday in Spain when he was performing at her hotel. She says her mind was dulled by the heat of the sun and the beat of the music and so she allowed him to sweep her off her feet. 'Don't make decisions when your feet are off the ground, Maria,' she told me. 'Especially when it comes to holiday romances.'

The only romance I'd ever had was when a boy in my class called Clarence gave me an 'engagement ring' in a decorated matchbox. That could hardly be called a 'holiday romance'. The ring was diamonds and emeralds. Pretend diamonds and emeralds, of course.

Our father put Charlie down and gave me a big bear hug.

'It's wonderful to see the two of you,' he said. 'You've

grown so tall, Maria! I've missed you both very very much! You can't imagine! It's been like a pain in my gut.' And he hunched over as if the pain was doubling him up now. He likes to act things out. My mother says I'm like him in that way. 'Stop dramatising, Maria!' she'll tell me and I'll tell her that I'm not *dramatising* and this is how I *feel*. I look like him, I know that, with my dark eyes and hair, while Charlie, being blond and blue-eyed, takes after our mother.

So we hugged and kissed and we laughed and he laughed, but I saw the tears in his eyes.

'Why didn't you come and see us before, Papa?' I asked.

'I have come – twice!' He held up two fingers. 'But you were never here. Last summer I wrote to ask your mother if I could see you but when I came you had gone. And she wouldn't tell me where.'

'She sent us up to Skye for the summer to stay with our cousins,' I said. 'How *dare* she do that! Not let us see you!' I had had no idea that he'd come. I had even been scolding him in my head for not coming when he'd promised, cross his heart, that he would. I'd cried when he hadn't come. I felt furious with my mother. I felt the rage building up inside me like a big, hot, rip-roaring fire. 'She'd no *right* to do that!'

'No right,' he agreed. 'After all, I am your father.'

Indeed he was.

The bell began to ring to mark the end of lunch break.

'Shall we go?' he said.

'Where?' I asked.

'Far, far away! Over the rainbow!'

'*Now*?'

'Why not!' he cried. 'Now is as good a time as any other. Do you know a better one?'

I didn't.

Papa's exciting. He makes you feel anything is possible. That is one of his attractions. I've heard my mother saying so to Aunt Heather, who, as you might guess, hasn't much time for excitement. She says it usually ends in tears.

'What about school?' I said, glancing back at the grey stone building and the swarm of children moving towards it. I saw Shona watching us from a distance. I'd said to her, 'There's my father!' before I'd gone dashing off to the gate so she would probably tell the teacher I was with him. I gave her a little wave and she gave a little unsure wave back and then turned away to speak to Amy.

'What about it!' cried Antonio, flinging wide his arms. 'Let's go!'

'And have a party?' said Carlos.

'And have a party!' said our father.

And so we went out of the school gate and along the street and round the corner to where he had a hired car waiting.

'Jump aboard!' he said.

We jumped.

'Where are we going?' I asked.

'Wait and see!'

Charlie and I sat on the back seat, strapped into safety belts that were an absolute necessity when our father was at the wheel, apart, of course, from being required by law. He's a skilful driver but he likes to drive fast. He was driving at breathtaking speed on this trip. I was certainly holding my breath and hanging on to the strap at the side of the car. He sang while he drove, at full throttle. His voice filled the car, drowning out sounds from the road. It was a flamenco song that he was singing. He's very intense when he sings as if it's coming from his heart, which it is. And when he's dancing he concentrates so hard that he sees no one in the room except his partner. And his feet move like magic.

'I am going to teach you flamenco, Maria!' he said when he had to slow for a light.

'I'd love that!'

'Me, too!' said Carlos.

'You too! We can be a family act.'

The light changed, and we moved on. I'd been so involved in watching my father drive that I hadn't had time to notice where we were going. I felt as if I was still inside my morning dream. Looking out of the window I saw a sign for the airport coming up.

'Are we going to the *airport*?' I asked.

'Is that where the party is to be?' asked Carlos.

'It is!' said our father. 'The beginning of it!'

He pulled in to the airport.

'Are we going to fly somewhere?' I asked.

'On a magic carpet!'

'Are we going for a holiday?' asked Charlie.

'The holiday of a lifetime!' said Antonio.

He parked the car in the car park and we got out.

'Quick, quick!' he said. 'We must hurry. We haven't got much time.'

He took off at a sprint and we followed at his heels. He

handed in the car key at the car rental desk and then he led the way to the check-ins.

I was beginning to feel a little uneasy. I wanted to go with him, I felt we had a right to go since *she*, our mother, had stopped us from seeing him. But I didn't want her to worry herself sick thinking we'd been kidnapped by some lunatic. On the other hand, it would serve her right since she hadn't played fair, either! My feelings were getting all jumbled up.

'Aunt Heather will wonder where we are.' I told my father that we were supposed to stay with her for a few days. 'She might go to the police.'

'I will phone her after we've checked in. You can give me her number.'

We joined a short queue. The board above the check-in woman's head said PARIS.

'Are we going to *Paris*?' I asked our father, but he hadn't heard. He was at the desk now, giving up his passport and our tickets for inspection. We are on his passport, Charlie and I, just as we are on Mum's British one. We have dual citizenship.

'Any luggage?' asked the woman.

'None,' said our father, except for a small bag he had in his hand which he would be able to take into the cabin. Charlie and I had nothing with us, not even a toothbrush. How could we go to Paris without any clothes other than the ones we were standing up in? Our father is bad in that way; he forgets about practicalities. I wondered if he would have any money to buy us new clothes. And how was he able to afford all these air fares? He must have been saving up.

The woman handed back the passport and three boarding passes. She said the plane would be boarding in a few minutes and that we should go directly to the departure gate.

'You are the last to check in!'

'But we made it!' Our father smiled at her.

I gave him Aunt Heather's number. He went to a phone and came back saying everything was fine. Aunt Heather had said to have a good time but I couldn't believe that! He doesn't *lie* exactly but he can be 'economical with the truth', as our mother puts it. So can she!

'Did you tell Aunt Heather we were going to Paris?' I asked.

He frowned as if he were trying to recall. 'It was so rushed, our exchange. I told her I had only a minute to spare. I said not to worry, I have you safe.' And then he would have put the receiver down and she'd have been rattling the buttons on her telephone trying to bring him back.

The voice over the loudspeaker, the one that calls the flights, was issuing its last and final boarding call for Paris. We had to run all the way. The departure lounge was empty.

'That was a close shave,' said the flight attendant when we reached the plane.

We hadn't been able to get three seats in a row, since we'd checked in so late, but our father soon sorted that. Using his charm he asked a woman if she would mind swopping.

'I would like very much to sit with my children,' he said. 'The little one is a bit nervous of flying.'

Charlie loves flying. He's always asking if he can go up to the cabin and sit beside the pilot. He wants to be an airline pilot when he grows up though there's plenty of time for him

11

to change his mind. He might even become a flamenco dancer! Our mother would have a blue fit if he did.

'Of course you must sit with your children,' said the woman, gathering up her magazines and paperback books and her handbag and a flight bag which had been stowed under the seat in front of her. Bits and pieces spilled from her in every direction and I helped pick them up.

'Thank you, dear,' she said, as if it was us that was doing her a favour.

'This is most kind of you, madam.' Our father made a short bow in her direction.

'That's perfectly all right,' she said, even though she was having to sit beside an enormous man with thighs like tree trunks that were spreading over on to her space.

We settled into our seats and fastened our seat belts. The plane took off dead on time.

'What will we wear in Paris?' I asked.

'Can I go to Euro Disney?' chirped Charlie. '*Please*, Papa!' His best friend had been there, and to Disneyland in Florida, which Charlie considered to be unfair.

'We shall not be spending long in Paris, children. We will merely be changing planes in the airport.'

I didn't ask where we would be going. I knew. Or at least I thought I did. But then, as you might have gathered, our father is unpredictable and full of surprises.

Three

There are no direct flights from Edinburgh to Spain. You either have to go to Glasgow where they have charters to Malaga and Alicante, and Gerona in the summer, or else by scheduled flight through Heathrow or Gatwick.

I knew straight away why our father had taken us through Paris. It would be to throw our mother off the scent. She wouldn't imagine we'd flown to France! It was only then that I fully registered that our father had snatched us. And that he must have planned it very carefully, which is unlike him. He usually acts on impulse. He must have wanted to do it very much.

In Charles de Gaulle airport he checked us in for a Madrid flight, whereas I had expected him to go to the Seville desk, or perhaps even Malaga. He lives in Seville. So he was being as roundabout as he could in order to lead our mother a dance! Maybe you couldn't blame him. After all, she was pretty sly herself sending us away from Edinburgh like that last summer. When I thought of it my blood boiled. I could feel it simmering underneath my skin.

In the departure lounge, while we were waiting for our flight to be called, our father said, 'You are going home! Home where you belong.'

'Just for a holiday, though?' I said. 'Not to stay?'

'We shall see.' He was smiling happily.

'You're not taking us away for good, are you, Papa?'

'Would you mind?'

'I don't know.'

'You are Spanish, Maria. Don't you feel it?'

'But I'm half Scottish as well. I feel that too.' I felt at home in Edinburgh, my mother's city, and I liked my school. I also liked my friends, especially Shona, my best friend.

'You were born in Spain,' said my father. 'It is in your blood. You are a Spanish citizen.'

Our parents had been arguing about this through the courts ever since they'd split up. A Spanish court had recently ruled that as Spanish citizens Charlie and I should live in Spain. My mother had told me, and added, 'Over my dead body. I'm not giving you up, no way!' She was in process of lodging an appeal. Aunt Heather says my mother tells me too much. She says it will make me old beyond my years.

We boarded the plane to Madrid. Half of me wanted to go, the other half did not. But we were on our way, I had to accept that. And because I couldn't do anything about it I let myself go floppy. I sank down into sleep. The excitement had worn me out and it felt great just to stop thinking for a bit.

When I awoke the fasten-your-seat-belts sign had come on and we were preparing for landing. My excitement returned. I felt as if I was in the middle of a great big adventure when you don't quite know what will happen next. I enjoy adventures, unlike Shona who prefers things to be the same

14

every day. She says she gets a flippy tummy when they're not. I tell her it's as well she wasn't born to parents like mine.

In a few minutes I'd be back in Spain. I had to admit that the thought pleased me.

'I knew you would want to come,' said Antonio. 'I knew it would make you happy.'

A friend of his was waiting for us in the airport. Pedro hugged the three of us in turn and said, 'Welcome home!'

Charlie was looking bewildered. He'd forgotten most of his Spanish; since he was four he had spoken English only. He hung onto my hand. I thought he might be about to start crying. It was all right, I told him, Pedro was an old friend of Papa's.

I remembered Pedro coming to visit us in Seville. It was while he was still a bachelor. He and our father had gone out to celebrate with some other friend whose wife had just given birth to a baby boy and they had come back very late, singing at the tops of their voices. They had rung the bell and wakened us all out of sleep and my mother had hit the ceiling. 'You Spanish men are so selfish,' she had screamed at them. 'You think of no one but yourselves.' It was one of many rows that our parents had. My mother says that they were temperamentally unsuited from the start. Her mother – my grandmother – says she told her that at the time but she wouldn't listen. I suppose when you're swept off your feet you might not hear properly.

We piled into Pedro's little car which I noticed had a couple of largish dents in the side. When he began to drive I could see why. He drove as if he was at the wheel of a dodgem car. He was even worse than our father, and that is saying something! And the traffic was ten times heavier than it is in Edinburgh, even in August when the big Arts Festival is on and the town is chock-a-block with tourists. As we swerved through the crowded Madrid streets I was aware of a lot of horn-honking and people shouting out of car windows. I hoped it wasn't all aimed at us. Two or three times we almost scraped the side of another vehicle. I held my breath until we were clear.

By the time we pulled up in Pedro's street I was feeling a little queasy.

'You are pale, little one,' he said, chucking me under the chin. I *hate* having my chin chucked. Though I did like Pedro. 'You need some Spanish sun,' he went on. 'In Scotland it never shines eh?'

'That's not true!' I said, pulling myself up. And I wasn't at all little. Everyone says I'm tall for my age. 'The sun often shines.'

But he wasn't listening. He was leading the way. He lived on the fourth floor of a dark tenement. We slogged our way up the rather smelly, gloomy stairs with Charlie whinging about being tired, which he probably was.

'You are a man,' our father told him. 'Men don't get tired.' But he did give him a piggy back up the last flight.

Pedro's flat was tiny. It consisted of two rooms, which he shared with his wife and two very small children.

'It's not a palace,' he declared. 'But you are most welcome to be our guests!'

Surely not to stay for our whole holiday! I glanced at my father but he was busy congratulating Lucia, Pedro's wife, on

16

her newest baby. 'He is so beautiful,' said my father. The child didn't look it to me. His head was a funny shape and his nose looked as if it had been made by slinging a lump of putty at his face.

Lucia kissed me on both cheeks. She felt a bit whiskery but she was also soft and pillowy and she welcomed us warmly.

'We do not have much,' she said, 'but it is yours to share.'

She was right, they didn't have an awful lot: a table, a few upright chairs, a splintered dresser, a settee and two armchairs which had the stuffing sticking out of them. I felt terribly snobby even to be thinking that. But the flat also smelt of garlic and wet nappies. Charlie was now sucking his thumb, which he hadn't done for ages. He snuggled close to me on one of the burst chairs.

Pedro was already bringing out a flagon of dark-red purplish wine. My father gave me a sip from his glass. That was enough! It tasted of vinegar and made my tongue smart but they didn't seem to mind. They drank one glass after another and soon came the singing. Pedro produced a guitar and gave me a maraca to shake. I began to enjoy myself. Even Charlie swayed a little, keeping time to the music.

After a while Lucia brought to the table a large iron casserole that had been cooking on the stove all evening. It smelt delicious. I was starving.

We went to the table and made a good meal of different kinds of beans cooked with tomatoes, onions, peppers and garlic, and little pieces of sausage. We mopped up our plates with heavy white bread and ate freely of the green and black olives from a dish in the centre. All of this was familiar to me,

17

though since returning to Scotland my mother had refused to make any kind of food that would remind us in any way of Spain.

Charlie ate very little. And he hardly spoke. His head drooped and he fell asleep slumped against the table. Our father lifted him up and carried him gently to the settee.

'You will not want to sleep, Maria!' he said. 'You are a night bird, like me.'

It was just as well that I was as there would have been nowhere to go to bed before Pedro and Lucia themselves did. They slept in the other room with their children.

Charlie was left to sleep on the settee with a blanket thrown over him. Later, much later, my father and I spread sheepskin rugs on the floor and lay down ourselves. Midnight had come and long gone by the time we were settled. I was so tired I could have slept on a slab of concrete.

Four

We were up early in the morning because of the baby. At first light he set up a wail which eventually turned to a roar. For one so small he could make a lot of noise. Then there was silence, while Lucia was feeding him. I was just drifting back into sleep when the older child, who was called Juan, also started to wail. He needed to go to the loo.

Pedro had to bring him through our room, the living room. 'Don't move,' said Pedro. 'We can step round you.'

As they passed Juan accidentally kicked me in the head. At least, I presumed it was an accident. Though, when I half opened an eye, I saw the little brat grinning.

After going to the loo Juan decided he was hungry. He made it plain that he was hungry. He wanted his breakfast. He *demanded* his breakfast.

'Yes, yes, I am going to get it, *rapido!*' said his father, trying to pacify him. Our mother says Spanish parents spoil their children. They allow them to stay up too late for one thing. She wouldn't have been one bit pleased if she'd seen me up till past midnight.

There seemed no point now in not getting up. I folded my sheepskin and went to the toilet. I sluiced my face with cold water and saw in the little spotted mirror above the sink that I

19

looked bug-eyed. I could have done with a shower. I was feeling pretty manky after travelling and sleeping in my clothes. But there was no shower. Or bath. When I asked Antonio how they got clean he said the children used the sink and Pedro and Lucia went once a week to her mother's for baths.

We had breakfast and then went shopping, Charlie, Antonio and I.

'We have to get you some clothes, do we not?' said our father.

'Can I have some new trainers?' asked Charlie. He's always bugging Mum for trainers and she won't buy him new ones until the old ones are falling to pieces. 'I'm not made of money!' she tells him. Nor, I was sure, was our father.

'Certainly you can have trainers!' he said. He said it in the kind of voice that suggested you could get anything in the world that you asked for. Charlie might believe him but I didn't. But it didn't matter that I didn't. I was happy to be with him.

It was sunny in the streets of Madrid. We walked, or rather strolled – for Antonio doesn't like to hurry – with him in the middle, holding our hands. It felt like being on holiday. We *were* on holiday. We stopped at a café. He drank coffee and we had ice cream. It was warm enough, just, to sit outside, with the sun on our faces. We watched the people going by until Charlie grew restless and started to swing his legs which meant that before long he kicked the table and upset Antonio's second cup of coffee.

'He doesn't like sitting,' I explained to our father, who had probably forgotten what small children are like.

We moved on.

'Shall we do our shopping now?' I said. I thought he might be capable of forgetting what we'd come out for. My school blouse and socks were grubby and the pleats in my skirt crumpled from a night on the floor. I could imagine my mother telling me that I looked a right ticket! I put her to the back of my mind. I felt wobbly when I thought of her.

We went into a department store.

'I don't have too much money,' our father warned us.

'That's all right,' I said.

'But enough?' asked Charlie anxiously.

'Enough,' said Antonio. 'We will always have enough.'

We spent a couple of hours raking through half the stock in the shop. Then we made our purchases. We each got an anorak, a pair of jeans, a change of underwear and socks, a pair of trainers (the cheapest there was, which didn't please Charlie), and two T-shirts. At home I had a drawerful of T-shirts. Mum says they only last a day. Like socks and knickers. With so few changes, it looked like somebody was going to have to do a lot of washing. I wondered who. Not me, surely! I'd never washed anything in my life. In Edinburgh we had a washing machine. There was no sign of one in Pedro and Lucia's flat.

'It cost me a lot for the fares,' said Antonio apologetically.

'Don't worry,' I said. 'We can get by for a week or two.'

I said that partly to see what his answer would be, but he didn't say anything. I then said, 'Papa, don't you think we should phone Mum to let her know where we are?'

'But she will come and try to take you away!' He was no

longer smiling. 'And then we'll have no time together. I haven't seen you for two whole years!'

'If I could just *speak* to her! I wouldn't tell her *exactly* where we are. I promise I wouldn't, cross my heart.'

He agreed that we could speak to her on the phone, both Charlie and myself, but we would just say that we were in Madrid and not mention Pedro. Not that she would know where Pedro lived or have any way of finding out. If she were to phone any of our father's relatives they wouldn't tell her. And Pedro wasn't in the telephone directory since he didn't have a telephone.

We rang from a call box. My hands felt clammy while we waited for the number to ring through. I hoped Mum wouldn't be too furious. I started to cough. I thought I might be about to choke.

There was a click, and the answering machine came on. My voice said, 'This is the answering machine for Fiona, Maria, and Charlie. We can't come to the phone right now but if you would like to leave a message please do so after the beep. Thank you.' It felt odd, listening to my own voice.

I heard the beep.

'What'll I say?' I asked Antonio.

'Tell her you are fit and well and having a good time.'

'Hello, Mum,' I said, clearing my throat noisily, 'this is Maria phoning from Madrid. We are with Papa and we are fit and well and enjoying our holiday. Don't worry about us. And please don't come to try to take us away. It's only fair that Papa should have some time with us.'

'Good girl!' said Papa.

I replaced the receiver. Our mother was in Seville by then, I learned later on, so she didn't get the message for a week or so. By which time we were no longer in Madrid.

Five

Next morning, our father announced that he was going to fetch his car. We were up early again and sitting at the table having our breakfast by seven o'clock, something I could never imagine doing back home.

'Where is it?' I asked. 'The car? You're not going to *Seville* to fetch it, are you?' I meant 'and leave us here.'

'It is here!' he said. 'In Madrid. Pedro has been keeping it in his garage while I was gone.' Pedro was a motor mechanic.

They set off together for Pedro's garage and Antonio returned alone half an hour or so later. His car was parked outside, the same old car he'd always had which my mother used to say was held together with string.

'Collect up all your things!' he said.

It didn't take long. We shoved our few clothes into plastic bags and were ready for off.

Lucia showered us with kisses and bade us *un buono viaje*. A good journey. 'Drive carefully!' she instructed our father. 'And not too fast.' As if his car could *go* fast. Lucia gave us a picnic of cheese and ham sandwiches and a slice of cold *tortilla* to eat en route.

'Restaurants are so expensive!' she said. And we wouldn't have money for them, that was for sure.

I was sorry to say goodbye to her. In two days I felt as if she'd become part of our family. I'd wondered what she thought of our father snatching us like that but she'd never said a word about it or mentioned our mother. She'd be loyal to him, I supposed.

We stumbled down the stairs into the brilliance of the street. It was going to be a sunny day.

'It still goes well,' said Antonio, patting the bonnet of his car affectionately. It might have been better if he hadn't spoken. He's good at tempting Providence.

He was going to let me sit in the front but Charlie made such a fuss that I had to sit in the back beside him to keep him quiet.

We headed south on the motorway. The road was busy but our little car chuntered happily along in the slow lane. Fast cars zipped past, and lorries with thundering great wheels. Our father sang. By midday the sun was in our eyes.

We pulled into a lay-by and ate our picnic, washing it down with warm lemonade. Then Antonio lay back with his hands behind his head and had a siesta. He always has a siesta, no matter what is happening. Charlie and I sat beside him watching the cars go by and inhaling the exhaust fumes. But our father would never think about that. Our mother would, though. I *had* to stop thinking what she would think.

Charlie grew bored so I started up a game of counting cars of different colours. I gave him red (so that he would win) and I took green. I wished we had some books with us but all our books were back in Edinburgh.

'What's Seville like?' asked Charlie.

'It's nice,' I told him. 'It has a cathedral with lacy bits round the top and orange trees in the streets. Sometimes the trees have blossom and fruit on them at the same time. They smell fabby.'

Charlie fancied the oranges and being able to reach up and pick one off but I wasn't sure if they'd be sweet enough to eat. 'I think they might be bitter like the kind they make into marmalade.'

We were talking about oranges when Antonio awoke. He sat up and stretched. He'd been asleep for an hour.

'I've been telling Charlie about Seville,' I said.

'Oh,' he said, not sounding very interested, then, 'Haven't you slept?'

'We don't sleep in the afternoon,' said Charlie.

'You have learnt bad habits!' said our father with a grin. 'You shall have to unlearn them.'

'Can we get on now?' I asked, trying not to sound impatient. Since we were on our way I wanted to get to Seville, to see our grandparents and our cousins. We had eight cousins and various aunts and uncles and great-aunts and great-uncles.

We got on, but only for a while, for the inevitable happened. We broke down. I remembered the car as always breaking down though I suppose that can't be totally true as sometimes we must have gone on journeys without anything going wrong.

The engine gave a warning cough and promptly died. Our father had a few things to say to it as he twisted and turned the ignition key and tried to urge it into life. But it was as dead as a doornail. Cars were swerving round us and sounding their horns. It was quite scary though Antonio didn't show any signs of alarm.

We had to push the car on to the hard shoulder.

'Now what?' I said.

'I shall have to mend it, won't I?' he said gaily.

He opened up the bonnet and his head disappeared inside it.

Two hours later, his hair on end and his hands covered in grease, he had to admit that he couldn't see what was wrong. 'We shall have to walk back to the nearest phone.'

We had to go with him. He wouldn't let us sit in the car and wait for him coming back. It wouldn't be safe.

'You mean somebody might kidnap us?' I said. I couldn't resist it.

'That's right!' he said, not taking it personally.

It was hot and dusty hiking along the motorway. Our new T-shirts were looking smutty already and again I wondered who would wash them. Grandmother perhaps. Or one of our aunts who had a washing machine. We made the phone call and trudged back to the car to await rescue.

We were towed into a garage in a nearby town where a mechanic set to work on our engine. An hour passed and he was still working. Our father paced worriedly up and down.

'What's wrong, Papa?' I asked.

'I don't know if I will have enough money to pay him.'

I should have known! Maybe the garage would keep the car until they got their money. Maybe we'd have to hitch the rest of the way to Seville. Maybe we'd just sit here all night on the tarmac.

The engine finally came back to life with a splutter and then purred smoothly.

'That's it!' said the mechanic, kissing the tips of his fingers.

My father followed him into the little glassed-in office. I saw Antonio waving his arms about and gesticulating at us. He would be spinning a sob story about his poor children. He must have been convincing for the bill was duly settled and our tank filled with petrol.

By this time it was getting dark and all the cars had their lights on. Charlie fell asleep soon after we were back on the road.

'Does Grandmother know we're coming?' I asked. I thought of one of Grandmother's big warm stews and my mouth watered. It seemed ages since we'd eaten our picnic. It *was* ages.

Antonio didn't answer. He seemed to be concentrating on the road.

'Is the car all right?' I asked.

'Going like a –'

'Don't say it!' I cried before he could get out the word 'bird'.

I saw that he was flashing his indicator to turn off the road.

'Why are you doing that?' I asked. 'Aren't we going to stay on the motorway all the way to Seville?'

'We are not going to Seville,' he said.

Six

A cloud moved over and the moon came out, half on its way to being full. It lit up the landscape where the lights of the car didn't reach. The earth looked bleached in moonshine but I knew it would be rusty-red by day and that the prickly pears and the other cacti would be olive green. The olive trees themselves looked black and scary with their branches making weird shapes like witches' arms against the night sky.

We were climbing upward. The road twisted and turned and began to narrow so that it was only one car-width wide. We saw headlights approaching, coming steadily towards us. It seemed like it was going to be a battle of wills as to which car would give way and back up. The other car was bigger and heavier than ours.

Swearing softly, Antonio backed up. I knew he would hate backing up. I felt our wheels shift and slide on soft gravel. I held my breath. Were we on the edge of a precipice? I couldn't see what was immediately on our right-hand side, only that there seemed to be a gloomy dark cavern and mountains beyond it. The headlights of the other car pursued us relentlessly.

We reached a passing space and Antonio backed into it. The other car swept past merrily tooting its horn.

'*Muchas grazias!*' said Antonio. Thank you very much!

He got out to take a closer look at the road. I followed him.

'It *was* a precipice,' I said in horror. 'And there are our skid marks. We could have toppled down there and been killed!'

'You exaggerate, Maria, my child! We were nowhere near death. I was in complete control all the time.'

I wondered if some cars had toppled over the brink and gone rolling, over and over, down to the very bottom.

'Listen, Maria, listen!' said my father. 'Listen to the silence of the mountains!'

We stood very still, he and I, listening. A night bird called, and a stone rolled somewhere, disturbed perhaps by a soft furry animal, but other than that it was very quiet. I could no longer be bothered to pester Antonio to know where we were going. He would not tell me till we arrived. And I no longer wanted to know until we did.

I got into the front seat beside him. Charlie was still sleeping in the back with his head sagging sideways and his mouth half open. The road remained narrow and we continued to climb upward into the heart of the mountains. My father sang more quietly now.

Up ahead, I saw the gleam of a white village. Was this to be our destination? It reminded me of the village I'd seen in my dream the night before our father came to take us away. What a long time ago that seemed!

We came to rest at the foot of the village.

'This is as far as we can go by car,' said Antonio, pulling the brake on tightly. 'There is only one small piazza up there and all the cars it will hold will be there already.'

'We have to walk?'

'We have to walk.'

First, we had to waken Charlie, who came up to the surface as if he had been deep down in sleep, living in a different life. He glanced wildly around him. He felt panicked. He didn't know where he was and it was dark.

'Mummy?' he shouted, thrashing around.

'Mum's not here,' I said, smoothing back his hair the way I'd seen our mother do. 'But I'm here, Charlie. Maria. And Papa's here.'

'Want Mummy!' He began to cry.

Papa took him into his arms. 'Don't cry, little one. You are going to be all right. You are with your Papa and your sister and in the morning the sun will shine and it will no longer be dark and you will see how beautiful are the mountains.'

We set off up the hill. Antonio had to carry Charlie so that meant I had to carry the plastic bags. I had to take three in each hand and before long I could feel the plastic cutting into my fingers.

The hill was very steep. I puffed and panted and had to rest from time to time and put down the bags. And each time we started up again I found it more and more difficult to thread my fingers through the hand-holds of the bags. Then one broke and our socks and knickers spilled on the ground. I sighed as I bent to pick them up.

'Soon be there,' said Antonio.

We reached the little piazza. It was indeed parked up with cars lying all higgeldy-piggeldy, not even pretending to be in straight rows. There was a church on one side of the piazza – washed white, of course, like everything else – and on another a café (closed, of course) and a shop (also closed). Houses formed the other two sides. I hoped it was one of those that we were making for.

'A bit further yet, I'm afraid,' said Antonio, as the church clock struck one.

The next part of the journey took us up an even steeper and yet narrower street. No cars could come beyond this point. The street was more of an alleyway and paved with cobble stones. I knew it was cobbled so that donkeys could get up and down without slipping. I had been in white villages before, but not this one. I felt pretty sure about that.

We went up and up as if we were about to ascend into heaven itself. I had to rest more and more often. My father urged me on.

'I know you're tired, Maria. But we're nearly there.'

We stopped just before the top. The ring of our feet on the cobbles had started a dog barking. The noise seemed horribly loud in the quietness. I thought it must waken the entire village but it seemed not. No shutters were thrown back. I wondered if anybody lived in this place, apart from the dog.

Our father set Charlie down and I let the bags collapse around my feet.

Antonio stood before a black wrought-iron gate. Beyond it ran a shadowy passageway. He tried the gate, rattling it slightly but firmly, but it didn't give way.

'Locked,' he said.

Would we have to spend the night in the street? Anything seemed possible.

'Whose house is this?' I asked.

'Great-aunt Teresa's. I don't think you ever met Great-aunt Teresa?'

'No,' I said, 'I didn't.'

'She never leaves the village,' he said, as if that explained it, and I supposed it did.

Teresa must be *his* great-aunt. That would mean she would be our great-great-aunt! She must be about a hundred years old!

'How are we to get in?' I asked.

'I shall ring the bell!'

He did, and we heard the peal of it coming from the end of the passage. Nothing else happened, except that the dog barked again.

'I'm shivery cold,' said Charlie, slipping a freezing hand into mine.

'She is quite hard of hearing,' said Antonio, ringing again. He then cupped his mouth with his hands and called out, 'Aunt Teresa! It's me – Antonio!' *Antonio*! His name echoed along the street.

Now somebody did throw a shutter back, but not Great-aunt Teresa. A man two houses up stuck his head out of the window and shouted, '*Callate*!' Quiet!

Antonio ignored him and rang the bell yet again several times in succession and yet again called on his great-aunt to come and let us in.

Eventually, she did. Through the whorls of black wrought-iron we saw an apparition in white appear at the end of the passage. Could it be a ghost? The ghost of Great-aunt Teresa? She might have died since Antonio had last clapped eyes on her. Charlie gripped my hand more tightly.

As the vision came closer we saw that it was a tiny old woman in a fluttery white nightdress. We were to find that during the day she wore nothing but black, like most of the other women in the village.

She pushed a large key into the lock and the gate creaked open.

'Antonio!' she cried, putting up her thin arms to him. 'I thought you were never going to come.'

So we had been expected.

Seven

The reason nearly all the women in the village wore black was that they were old or getting to be old. I had thought they must be widows but Antonio said that not all of them were. Quite a few, however, had managed to live longer than their husbands. Hardly anyone in the village was young. The only other child was a baby of nine months.

Great-aunt Teresa was a widow. Antonio said her husband had died so long ago that she looked vague if you mentioned him. I didn't think I would ever have reason to mention him.

I awoke that first morning to find myself in a small white-washed room with Charlie lying in the other narrow bed beside me. A bleached blue curtain covered the window. I jumped up and pulled it back.

The view would have blown your breath away. I looked down over the jumbled collection of red-tiled roofs to the countryside beyond, to the line after line of high sierras fading away into the distance in a bluish haze. Looking out from up here was like being in a fortress. For some reason I thought of Bluebeard locking his wife away in a high tower. But that was ridiculous! My father wasn't Bluebeard and we weren't prisoners. I could open the door and walk straight out of here. But where would I go?

We were in the middle of nowhere. I said so to Antonio when he came into the room to see if we were awake.

'Everywhere is in the middle of somewhere,' he said.

'But you know what I mean!'

He smiled. He didn't seem to know or, if he did, he wasn't letting on. He said, 'You used to like white villages. You liked to hop up and down the streets.'

'I was younger then.'

That made him smile again. 'Only by two years.'

To me that seemed quite a long time.

Charlie awoke, and we went through to the living room to have breakfast, although it was actually lunchtime. We had slept for ten hours, which wasn't surprising considering what the day before had been like.

Kitted out in her black, Aunt Teresa (we had to drop the 'great' as it got too much to keep saying) was sawing a piece of bread off a hard-looking white loaf. Her hands were gnarled and her face resembled a chestnut that had been left out in the sun. I took a hunk of bread. At home in Edinburgh we ate only brown. Our mother says white isn't good for you. I decided not to point that out.

Neither Charlie nor I were very hungry. We nibbled at the bread and drank the hot chocolate Antonio brewed up for us. Aunt Teresa clucked, making a noise a bit like a hen.

'Children need to eat more!' she said, waving her bent little hands around. 'You will never grow tall.'

Considering I was nearly a full head taller than her I didn't think she had a leg to stand on. I leaned back and studied the room.

It was a nice room, I had to admit, with its rust-coloured, flagged floor, and its walls decorated half way up with green, yellow and blue tiles. The floor-length window was open on to a wrought-iron balcony in which geraniums and pansies made a real riot of colour. Antonio was to sleep in this room as there was only one other bedroom, which was Aunt Teresa's. But there was a bathroom with a bath and a flushing loo and I was glad of that.

When we'd finished eating Antonio, Charlie and I went out to explore.

Most of the houses seemed to have been newly washed white. They shone in the afternoon sunshine. And nearly all had flowers on their balconies.

'Pretty, aren't they?' said Antonio. 'I am very fond of this village. It has not been ruined by tourist shops selling touristy things. Like flamenco dancers that turn out to be salt cellars!'

I didn't imagine many tourists would find their way here.

Every few yards we were stopped by women in black. Some sat on hard chairs in front of their doors, others were propping up the walls chatting to neighbours. They must have been glad when they saw us coming! It might be the biggest event of their day.

'Antonio!' They got off their chairs to greet him. They seemed fond of him. They hugged and kissed him and made jokes about his appearance. He'd grown even more handsome than when they'd last seen him!

'And are these your children?'

They turned their attention to us. It was Charlie whom they fell in love with.

What beautiful hair he had! Just look at his golden curls! It would not be often that they saw such golden curls! What beautiful blue eyes he had! Like cornflowers in spring. Everyone around had dark eyes, including me.

'And this is Maria?'

Yes, I acknowledged, I was Maria.

'And what age are you, Maria?'

'Eleven,' I said.

'She is a big girl for eleven, Antonio,' they said.

'I am almost twelve,' I said. 'I will be twelve in five months time.'

By the time we reached the piazza below Charlie had been pawed over by a number of women but he didn't seem to mind. Antonio said we should rest ourselves by taking a little refreshment at the café. Half the men in the village were already sitting there, lapping up the warmth of the sun. They sat there most of the day. Their wives didn't want them cluttering up the house.

They all greeted Antonio, who was obviously well known to them.

He ordered a small cup of strong black coffee and Charlie and I had a freshly-made lemon drink. The proprietor put our drinks on tick which worried me as I wasn't sure when our father would manage to pay. I wasn't confident, either, that Aunt Teresa would have much more money than he had.

The proprietor, whom our father called Diego, joined us at our table.

'So, Antonio,' he said, 'how long will you be staying with us?'

I perked up my ears at that. I wanted to know the answer to that question too.

'I'm not sure,' said Antonio. 'It depends.'

Diego nodded. 'On your work eh? Have you some engagements coming up?'

'A few. In fact, I have to go down to the coast tomorrow for a couple of days.'

'Well, needs must!' said Diego. 'We all have to earn our living. You'll soon learn that too, Maria.'

'I am only eleven,' I told him. 'Though I am going on twelve.'

'You are big for twelve, Maria,' he said.

When he went off to serve another customer I said, 'How does he know what is big for twelve? No one round here *is* twelve! Everyone is ninety-nine going on a hundred!'

'I believe there is a girl of twelve down in the valley,' said my father.

'Down in the valley!' I scoffed. 'One girl of twelve!'

'I know her grandmother.'

'Bully for you!'

'Don't be sharp, Maria! It doesn't suit you. You sounded like your mother there.'

'You are going to take us with you, though, aren't you?' I asked. 'To the coast?'

'I'm afraid not,' he said, confirming my fears. 'I cannot, Maria! I have to work. There would be nowhere for you to stay.'

'But what are we to do?'

'Why, you will stay with Aunt Teresa,' he said.

Eight

I argued with him and when that got me nowhere I had a tantrum. Even girls of eleven can have tantrums at times.

'It's not fair snatching us like that and then leaving us locked up in this white prison with your ancient old aunt! If you leave us here and don't take us with you I shall run away and take Charlie with me and go back to Scotland and never set foot in Spain ever again!'

Charlie began to cry.

'Now look what you're doing!' said our father, putting his arm round Charlie. I had waited until we got back to Aunt Teresa's. I wouldn't have started rowing with him in public with all those women in black flapping their ears and shaking their grizzled heads.

'It's not what *I'm* doing,' I said to our father. 'It's what *you've* done!'

'Maria,' he said, 'you can be so grown-up –'

'Oh, yes, I know – for my age!'

'Yes, for your age. But now you are sounding like a baby.'

I aimed a hard round cushion at his head but he fielded it with one hand.

'Now, Maria, my love, calm down.'

'You don't *love* me! How can you when –'

'I'll leave you for two days? I have to, I tell you! I shall be working until one o'clock in the morning.'

'You kept us up till one o'clock *this* morning, because it suited you!'

'It did not *suit* me! It just happened! I did not *arrange* for the car to break down.'

'I hope it breaks down on the way to the coast! On the edge of a precipice!'

'Thank you for that nice wish! You would like to see your Papa dead, would you?'

Charlie set about crying again.

'Why can't you just *take* us?' I asked. 'Charlie doesn't want you to go either, do you, Charlie?'

'When I finish work each night I shall have to sleep on a friend's floor,' said Antonio, trying to sound patient, though I could see that he wasn't really, underneath. 'You can't sleep on his floor.'

'Why not?' I demanded.

And so we went on until he made me a promise. The next time he had to go down to the coast for an engagement he would take us with him.

'Promise? Cross your heart?'

He crossed his heart. He also promised that he would bring me back some books to read. Preferably in English, I requested. 'And not too babyish.' He'd have no idea what a girl of almost twelve would be reading. There was an English bookshop where he was going, he said. He would ask their advice. If I didn't get something to read soon I would frizzle up with boredom, I told him. It was all very well talking about

41

exploring the village, but you couldn't explore it for ever, could you? And certainly not after dark when you were lying in bed unable to sleep.

So he made his promises. And the next morning he left for the coast.

The house felt empty without him. I mooched about not knowing what to do. Charlie was along the street being fed almond cakes and marzipan sweets by one of the women in black. I'd told him he'd rot his teeth if he went on eating so much sweet stuff.

'I'll get new teeth,' he'd said, grinning and showing me his gap at the front.

'Two days will soon pass,' said Aunt Teresa. 'Your father had to go for the work, Maria. He needs the money.'

She didn't have to tell me that.

She asked me to go to the shop to get bread and onions. At least it would be something to do. A fresh loaf was a good idea. The old one was a strain on the teeth and there was blue mould round its edges.

'And some cheese!' said Aunt Teresa. 'We could do with some cheese.'

'What kind?'

'What kind? They have only one kind.'

I waited for her to give me some money but she made no move to lift her saggy old leather purse that lay on the dresser. Maybe it was saggy because there was nothing in it.

'I suppose I'll have to pay,' I said.

'Tell them Antonio will pay when he comes back from the coast.'

I hated having to take messages like that. Josefa, who was Diego's wife and ran the shop, didn't seem bothered. She marked down the amount in a battered notebook. The pages were covered with figures. I squinted, trying to see if there were any more under Antonio's name but I couldn't make out her writing.

'How do you like being in our village, Maria?' asked Josefa, as she weighed up the cheese, taking her time.

'Fine,' I said.

She laid the piece of cheese on a piece of paper and wrapped it, also taking her time.

Of course if you live in a place like this there is all the time in the world to weigh and wrap cheese. But I had the feeling that she also wanted to keep me here.

'And how is your mother?' She gave me a sly look. I didn't know what she would know, what any of them would know.

'Fine,' I said.

'Is she coming back to Spain?'

'Perhaps,' I said.

I put the bread and onions and cheese into the plastic bag Aunt Teresa had given me.

'*Adios*,' I said.

Josefa had brought my mother back into the front of my mind. I had been trying to keep her at the edge. I longed to speak to her, to hear her voice. Why shouldn't I speak to her! There was a telephone box in the piazza. I would phone and tell her where we were and she could come out and join us and cut our holiday with Antonio short. It would serve him right if she were to come! Then he'd realise he should have taken us with him to the coast.

I crossed the piazza and went into the phone box, watched by the old men sitting outside the café. Most of the time they didn't drink anything, they just sat. Josefa was probably watching from the shop window as well and wondering whom I could be phoning. Let her wonder! Diego had now come to his door and was leaning against the jamb. Let them all wonder! I kept my back to them.

Then I remembered that I had no money! And I had no way of getting any. There was no point in rummaging in the bottom of my pockets because I didn't even have a peseta.

I presumed I could reverse the charges, even though it was for an international call. My mother had always told me to reverse the charges if I found myself stranded. Well, I was stranded now. I dialled the operator.

He sounded very nice and sympathetic when I told him that I was stranded here in Spain in the middle of nowhere and that I needed to let my mother in Scotland know where I was since she would be going round the bend with worry. He said he could understand that! He asked me for the number and I said it slowly and clearly so that there would be no mistake. I didn't want to be put through to the wrong number! He asked also for my name and my mother's name and I gave him those too.

'One moment, please,' he said.

My heart was thudding. The number was ringing, all the way from Edinburgh to the middle of nowhere in Spain. And then I heard that infuriating click and the answering machine coming on with my voice chanting, 'This is the answering machine for Fiona, Maria and Charlie. We can't come to the phone right now but if you would like to leave a message please do so after the beep. Thank you.'

I wanted to scream at my own voice. I asked the operator if I could leave a message.

'I'm very sorry,' he said, 'not without someone accepting the charges for the call. But I could put you through to the police without any charge. They would be the best people to help you contact your mother. I really think that is what you should do!'

Nine

I put down the receiver so quickly that it slipped from my fingers as if buttered and I had to make a lurch to retrieve it. In doing so I banged the edge of my head on the shelf. I glanced round. The eyes in the piazza were still trained on me. I took a deep breath and counted to ten, the way my mother had taught me to do in a panic. Keep cool, calm and collected, is her motto. The three cs. I didn't feel all that calm after I'd got to ten, or particularly collected.

I couldn't possibly phone the police and have them arrive at Aunt Teresa's to arrest Antonio. But the operator might decide to phone them himself. He might ring and say, 'I've just been talking to a young girl who said she was stranded and was trying to contact her mother in Scotland to come and rescue her.' He would be able to give the number of the phone box and they would know that it was situated here, in this village. It wouldn't take a lot of detective work to find that out.

I left the phone box and walked as briskly as I could up the hill, allowing for the steepness of the incline and the rough going underfoot. Cobbles are not made for speed. Especially when donkeys have deposited their droppings on them. I didn't look back.

'Your face is pink like a peony,' said Aunt Teresa, who was

sitting outside her door on an upright chair.

'It's the hill,' I said.

'That is why I seldom go down,' she said. 'For then you have to come up.'

'How do you get your shopping?' I asked. 'When we aren't here?' And then I remembered! I'd left the bag in that stupid old phone box!

'There is always someone going up and down,' said Aunt Teresa. She leaned forward to peer at my hands and then at the ground round my feet. She frowned. 'Where is the shopping?'

I told her I'd left it, not in the phone box of course, but in the shop. Near enough. Not too big a white lie. 'I'll go back for it now. Straight away!'

Before she could start lamenting I turned and went shuttling back down to the piazza, zigzagging round the narrow, twisty streets, taking care not to slip and sprain my ankle. My temple was throbbing a little from the bump against the telephone shelf. I met a donkey half way down with a wide load of firewood straddling its back. I had to lean against the wall to avoid being scratched.

Out of breath, I reached the piazza. All the old men were still sitting there. But there was no sign of any policeman.

I went into the phone box. It was empty! I did a double-take, but there was nothing on the floor except for a squashed cigarette packet and a stubbed-out cigarette. The shopping must have taken legs and walked, or been uplifted. I hardly thought a thief would have chanced to come by and grab it. I opened the door and stepped outside.

47

'Josefa's got it,' one of the old men called over to me.

I went to the shop.

'Ah, Maria!' said Josefa. 'You left your bag in the phone box!'

Just give it to me! I said inside my head. But I knew she wouldn't, not without taking the chance to pry.

'You were calling your father?' she said.

'No.'

'I didn't think you could be. You wouldn't know where he'd be exactly, would you?'

'No.'

'Did you get through with your call?'

'No.'

'That was a pity! Somebody would be disappointed?'

I lifted my shoulders in a Spanish shrug. She didn't quite have the nerve to ask me outright whom I'd been trying to call. She passed over the shopping.

Walking back up the hill it came to me that the police would not arrest Antonio even if they were to come. The law would be on his side, for the Spanish court, after all, had ruled that we were to live in Spain. It was my mother who could be arrested if she were to come and try to snatch us back.

The best thing would be to have a good holiday here with Antonio and then talk him into letting us go quietly back to Scotland. He loved us so I didn't see why he would want to make us unhappy by keeping us against our will. He was not a bad man. Or an evil man.

When I got back up to our level I found Aunt Teresa deep in talk with a neighbour. When they saw me they broke off and the other old woman hobbled back into her house giving me a backward look.

Aunt Teresa and I went inside.

'I hope I got the right amount of cheese.' I said, unpacking it.

'Whom did you phone?' she asked. Pigeon Post must have been in operation! Or did the neighbour have a telephone and, if so, had Josefa phoned and told her to pass the message along? Tittle-tattle, tittle-tattle! It was a pity their tongues couldn't get caught in a mincer.

'No one,' I said, laying the bread and onions on the table beside the cheese.

'You phoned someone,' insisted Aunt Teresa, picking up one of the onions to sniff. She had a habit of sniffing food. To see if it was off, I supposed. Unfortunately mouldy bread doesn't smell. 'You were seen speaking to someone in the phone box,' she said.

'I like talking to myself! Is it illegal for someone of my age to go into a phone box?'

'Your father will want to know about this.'

'And you no doubt will tell him!'

'It is my duty, Maria. He put you in my charge.'

It was more like *I* who should be in charge of *her*! She couldn't see beyond a few yards and kept burning pots and threatening to set the house on fire. Perhaps even the whole village. The houses were so hugger-mugger close together that a flame might lick along from one to the other in no time. Then it would spread like wildfire! I could see it all. My mother used to say I over-exercised my imagination at times.

Used to say! Why did I think that way? As if she belonged to our past lives. But of course she would still be in our lives for years and years to come and saying all sorts of things to us, good and bad!

My ancient relative in the fusty black dress might not be able to see too well, but there was nothing wrong with the tongue in her head, for all of her eighty-seven years.

'I have to tell him,' she repeated. 'It is my duty.'

'That's if he comes back for you to tell him,' I said. If Antonio kept his promise he should return tomorrow. Only two nights away, he'd said. 'I bet he doesn't! Not when he promised.'

And he didn't.

'A day here or there means nothing to a man like Antonio,' said his great-aunt complacently.

A man like Antonio! You'd have thought he was a god!

Ten

When Antonio didn't come after two nights I said, 'I told you so!'

'Patience, my child,' said Aunt Teresa. 'It is good to learn patience early in life.'

So that when you were old you could sit patiently on a chair outside your front door waiting for something to happen?

I felt gloomy deep down inside. What if our father were to stay away for two weeks? For two months? For ever? We would be left rotting away up here in this white fortress, forgotten.

People might ask him, 'Antonio, I thought you had two children?'

'Two children?' he would say, frowning, racking his brains. 'I believe I once did have two children. Yes, a girl and a boy! The boy was called Carlos and the girl – Let me see now! What *was* her name? How stupid of me but I can't quite remember! But, yes, you're right, I once did have children. I must have mislaid them.'

He might have had an accident (who'd be surprised, driving the way he does?) and be lying unconscious in a hospital down on the coast. They would find papers in his pocket giving his address in Seville and they would notify his family there. No

51

one would know that we were here. I didn't think any of them came often to visit Aunt Teresa.

'Antonio is *using* you,' I told Aunt Teresa.

'*Using* me?'

'Yes, by parking us on you.'

'I am pleased to have Antonio's children.'

There was no use trying to talk to Aunt Teresa. He would never do any wrong, in her eyes, even if he were to rob a bank.

I sat out on the balcony mulling over all the possible scenarios and planning, if Antonio did not come back, how Charlie and I would make our escape and head down to the coast. We could hitch rides. There, my imagination faltered. Our mother had dinned into us since babyhood that we should never *ever* take a ride in a stranger's car. She'd made it sound so dreadful that I didn't think I could actually do it. I didn't want to be murdered and dumped by the roadside.

Another option would be to get hold of some money and phone our grandmother in Scotland, or even Aunt Heather. I stopped there again. How would I get the money? By *stealing* it? Thou shalt not steal. I knew all that, but this was a desperate situation where the rules didn't seem to apply. But whom could I steal it from? Aunt Teresa didn't appear to have any, unless she kept it close to her body. Sewn inside her woolly vest perhaps? The only person I'd seen handling money in the village was Josefa. I couldn't see myself knocking her on the head and robbing the till. Nor did I imagine anyone would *lend* me money to make a phone call. I shelved that set of thoughts for the moment.

Sitting there perched high above the valley I watched the road below hoping for the sight of Antonio's little red car. The trouble was that there were dozens of little red cars similar to his. Well, maybe not *dozens*, for it is not a busy road, to tell the truth, but two or three. The cars looked like Dinky toys creeping up the narrow ribbon of road to the village.

Each time I saw a small red car I jumped up and hung over the balcony until Aunt Teresa came out to prevent me falling to my death.

'You'll kill yourself!' she cried, clamping her twiggy fingers round my ankles and almost making me go over with the shock. 'It is a long way down.'

She was right about that. I slid back down into my chair.

It must have been then, when I took my eyes off the road, that Antonio's car passed below. Twenty minutes later, while I was still scanning the road, I heard Aunt Teresa's voice rising on a note of delight.

'Antonio!' she was crying.

And there he was, as handsome as ever, without even a sling on his arm or a strip of sticking plaster on his forehead to suggest he'd had an accident. He was smiling. I flung myself into his arms.

'Papa,' I cried, 'where have you been?'

'The car broke down! I had to stay an extra night while it was fixed.'

That sounded reasonable enough. I didn't want to challenge it, anyway. I was just happy to have him back. And he'd even remembered my books! He took them from his knapsack and gave them to me.

I tried not to show my disappointment. He'd brought me two Enid Blytons which I'd read when I was eight, almost four years ago.

'Thank you, Papa,' I said.

'You're pleased with them?'

'They're a *bit* young for me, but I'll read them. Yes, I will!'

And I did, that night, in bed. At least I read one from beginning to end and I could remember how it did end so there weren't any surprises in it. But it was good to have *something* to read before I went to sleep.

Before going to bed, though, we had a special meal to celebrate Antonio's return. He had brought a chicken home with him. By the time Aunt Teresa had cleaned and roasted the bird it was late. But then they were used to eating late.

'It's not a bad thing to go away sometimes,' said Antonio, as we sat at the table. His eyes twinkled. 'For then everyone is pleased to see you come back.'

'But you won't go away again, will you?' I said.

At that point we heard the door rattle, and in shuffled Aunt Teresa's neighbour, the one with the telephone. Nobody locked their doors here so they could go in and out of one another's houses without knocking.

'Telephone for you, Antonio,' she said.

While he was away I felt anxious.

'Eat up your chicken now, Maria,' chided Aunt Teresa. 'It is a good fresh bird. It must only have been slaughtered this morning. I could tell by the giblets when I was cleaning it.'

I wished she hadn't said that. I pushed my plate away. I had almost decided to become vegetarian before we left home. Left home! How long ago was that? I couldn't remember. The days had seemed to run into one another, with nothing to mark one out from the other, except that tomorrow was going to be Sunday and we would go to mass in the little white church on the piazza. It was the only time that Aunt Teresa made the journey down to the lower part of the village. She made it sound like a trip to the south pole. I wondered if she'd take oxygen along.

Antonio came back. We looked at him expectantly.

'Who was it?' asked Charlie, who had been eating his chicken with gusto. He hasn't yet come to realise meat comes from dead animals. 'Was it Mummy?'

There was a minute's silence so that everyone could recover from him asking the question straight out like that, then our father said, 'No, it was a friend.'

'What kind of friend?' asked Charlie. 'Was it Pedro?'

'Pedro doesn't have a phone,' I said, my eyes fixed firmly on Antonio.

'It was someone I perform with,' he said, taking a drink of wine.

'A dancer?' I asked. 'Or a singer?'

'A singer,' he said.

'Is it a she?' asked Charlie. This was getting to be like I-Spy. Someone beginning with S. Which turned out to be right. S, I would come to learn, stood for Sylvana.

'Yes,' said Antonio, 'it was a she.' He drained his glass.

'What did *she* want?' asked Charlie. (It is useful having a small brother at times.)

'She wanted to tell me that we have another couple of engagements.'

'Down on the coast?' I asked.

'Yes, I'm afraid so,' he said, and poured himself another glass of wine. 'That is where the money is.'

That did it! If he didn't let me go with him this time I was definitely going to take Charlie and run away. We would just have to take our chances on being murdered.

Eleven

I didn't raise the subject straight away. I decided to wait until tomorrow, after we'd been to church. If he'd just come from church his conscience might be worrying him and he wouldn't want to upset me a second time.

After church, everyone stood around on the piazza for a while talking. Some of the men drifted over to the café to drink a small brandy. Antonio was among them. He seemed to be buying drinks for half the other men with his newly-earned money.

'I hope he keeps some,' muttered Aunt Teresa, speaking my thoughts for me. 'He can be too generous.'

'Maria!' Josefa was signalling to me. She had been in the congregation. Her shop was shut today.

I started guiltily. But she couldn't have known that I'd been debating whether I could knock her on the head and raid her till. I went reluctantly across to her. But she only wanted to introduce me to the twelve-year-old girl who lived in the valley.

'Maria,' said Josefa, 'this is Paula.'

We both said, '*Hola!*' Hello. And that was the only word I heard Paula speak that day. She stood on one leg, sort of twisting the other round it, a bit like a stork. She seemed gawky and rather shy. Josefa did the talking for us.

'You two girls must become friends!' Saying that was enough to make us take a dislike to one another on the spot. Paula was staring at her feet. It hadn't taken me long to mark Josefa down as a real bossy boots and far too interfering. She went on, 'Maria, you could go and visit Paula. She lives on a farm just three kilometres away. A big girl like you could easily walk three kilometres.'

What about a girl like Paula? She *was* smaller and thinner than me. Maybe that was why Josefa thought I should be the one to do the walking. Somehow I didn't think we'd have much in common, other than being around the same age. Which everyone knows isn't enough. But I thought the contact might come in useful. She might even be able to lend me some money for a phone call if I needed it.

'I'd like to come and visit you, Paula,' I said, and she looked up. 'But I can't this week, I'm afraid. I'm going down to the coast with my father for a few days.'

Paula just goggled at me. She'd probably never been to the coast to see all the high-rise touristy hotels which my father hates. He says they have spoiled the beautiful coastline of his country.

'But he has just come back,' said Josefa.

'I know,' I said loftily, 'but some other engagements have cropped up. He had a phone call last night.'

'Indeed?' said Josefa, hoping no doubt for more details, which I did not intend to give her. I didn't know them myself, other than that the singer was a she.

I said, '*Adios,*' to Paula and Josefa and went back to rejoin my great-great-aunt and my brother. Charlie had his mouth full. Again!

'You shouldn't let him eat so many sweets, Aunt Teresa,' I said. 'Our mother will be furious if he comes back with his teeth rotted.' I looked Aunt Teresa in the eye daring her to say we were not going back.

Charlie made a cheeky face at me and opened his mouth to show how full it was. Never mind his teeth, these women would have *him* spoiled rotten before they were done!

Our father got up and came over to claim us. He gave Aunt Teresa his arm and we set off on the return journey. Aunt Teresa looked very pleased with herself, having her tiny hand tucked into the crook of his strong arm. She greeted everybody on the way up, making sure that they saw her with Antonio. Charlie and I came behind like two attendants at a wedding.

We lunched on chicken left-overs and tomato and black olive salad and then Aunt Teresa went off to have her siesta. We heard her start to snore two minutes after she'd shut the door of her room. Antonio looked as if he might be about to drop off too but I wanted to speak to him while Aunt Teresa was asleep. Charlie had disappeared into another widow-woman's house. She had a collection of toy cars that her son had had when he was a child which she was going to pass on to him.

'Papa?' I began.

'Yes?' He yawned.

'Please take me with you this time when you go to the coast!'

'Now, Maria –'

'Now, Papa!' I could feel my temper rising. 'Why did you bother to come and snatch us if you weren't going to be with us half the time?' It seemed like a good question to me. He seemed to think so too as he took a minute or two to consider it.

'I didn't *know* that I would be away so much then.' He sat up, fully awake now. 'Maria, did you phone your mother when I was away?'

'Would it be a crime if I did?'

'No, but you know what we agreed? Not to let her know where you are in the meantime. Until we have some time together.'

'That's just it! We're not having any time.'

He sighed and admitted that I had a point. 'All right then! You can come!'

'You really mean it?'

'I really mean it.'

I jumped up and gave him a hug.

'By the way,' he said, 'did you get through to your mother?' He'd tried to sound as if he wasn't bothered whether I had or not, but I knew that he must be.

'No.'

He nodded, as much as to say, 'That's all right.' His eyelids were sinking.

'Papa,' I said, 'what is your singer called?'

'Sylvana,' he said and closed his eyes, closing also the conversation.

Twelve

I was excited about going off with my father on another trip.
Charlie was asked if he would like to come too but he said he
didn't want to spend hours and hours in a boring old car feeling
sick. Also, he was getting used to the old women fussing over
him and popping sweets into his mouth!

'Bring me a present back!' he said.

Aunt Teresa was not too pleased at my going. I heard her
say to my father that this could prove to be a big mistake.

'You will regret it, Antonio!'

'Why should I?' He was not in the mood to listen. He had
been whistling a cheerful little tune and now he took it up
again. I smiled. I was going to have him all to myself on this
journey.

We set off the next day, taking the packets of thick
sandwiches which Aunt Teresa pressed upon us. We sang for
the first hour, until we both became hoarse.

We had a good drive without any incidents. We tootled
along in the slow lane except when Antonio got the engine
wound up to pass a long lorry. The car was behaving itself
splendidly though neither of us made the mistake of saying so.
We made one stop to eat our sandwiches and drink from a
bottle of water.

'I like travelling,' I said as we sat in a lay-by watching the other traffic whiz past.

'There's a bit of the gypsy in you!' said Antonio. 'You take after me.'

His mother – my grandmother – was a true gypsy and when she was younger she used to sing flamenco. She still sings, at home, that is, and her voice is strong and carrying. Or she did when I last saw her.

'When am I going to see Grandmother?' I asked. 'And Cousin Rosa?' Rosa was my special friend in Seville.

'When it is time,' said Antonio, gathering up the lunch papers. 'Let's get back on the road!'

We moved down closer and closer to the coast. The orange and apricot trees were blossoming and there were masses of wild flowers along the roadside making gorgeous splashes of yellow and pink and white. Spring was further on here than up in the village, which was a long way above sea level.

At last, we sighted the sea.

'Look!' cried Antonio. 'There it is – the Mediterranean!'

Gradually the line of blue-green widened and then we were running along by the side of the sea itself and I could hear the waves as they curled in on the sand. There are no tides in the Mediterranean so the sea is always close in to the shore, which I like. I hate miles of mud flats.

I wound down my window and let the breeze ruffle my hair. The sun was low down in the western sky but still shining. Holidaymakers had been lying on the beach even though it was still only March. They were packing up their towels and straw mats. Evening was coming in. It's Antonio's favourite time of day. Mine too. I can't wait till I'm grown up and able to stay up till midnight every night.

Our first stop was to be in a place called Torre del Mar. I didn't like it on sight!

'I knew you wouldn't,' said Antonio cheerfully.

It seemed to be made of nothing but very ugly high rises but I didn't complain. I was happy just to be there.

He had booked a room in a farmhouse on the outskirts of the town. The farmer's wife seemed to know him well and kissed him and then me on both cheeks. 'So this is your daughter from Scotland!' she said. Everyone in Spain seemed to know Antonio and his business.

She fed us a meal of boiled potatoes and fried sardines, which I am not overly fond of because of the bones, but I ate it all up so as not to offend her. Afterwards, Antonio and I lay down on the single beds in our room and slept for a couple of hours so that he (and I) would be refreshed for the evening's performances. He was to do the first one at ten and the second at eleven after a fifteen-minute break.

The shows were to take place in the dining room of a hotel. People were still finishing off their meal when we arrived. They sat at long tables making me think of school dinners in my Edinburgh school. The room smelt of food, of course. How could it not? I wondered if that wouldn't put Antonio off.

'Nothing puts me off once I start to dance!' he said.

I was waiting to meet Sylvana with some trepidation. She would be beautiful no doubt with scarlet lips and sleek black hair pulled smoothly back into a knot.

The performers were given a little cubby-hole to change in. A woman was in there already, dressed in a black and white spotted dress, all flouncy round the bottom in true flamenco style. She greeted Antonio in the way that everyone else did, as if he was their bosom pal and they hadn't set eyes on him for ten years.

'Maria,' said Antonio, breaking out of the embrace, 'I want you to meet Sylvana.'

'Maria!' she said, giving me a wide smile, and then, as to be expected, she swooped in on me to plant kisses on my cheeks.

I couldn't help gawking at her for she wasn't young and beautiful at all. She was old, not as old as Aunt Teresa and her pals, but quite old. About fifty, I thought, though I'm not very good at guessing the age of anyone over twenty-one. I felt relieved. What a twit I'd been getting all steamed up and jealous of her in advance!

'Are you looking forward to our show?' she asked. She really seemed very nice.

'Very much!' I said. 'Papa says you have a very fine voice.'

'Ah,' she said with a laugh, 'he is a flatterer, your Papa!'

Someone else was approaching. We heard a flurry of light footsteps at the door and turned.

'Maria,' said my father, 'I want you to meet Carmen! She is the other dancer in our little troupe. She is my partner!'

There was a light in his eye that told me quite a lot. My spirits dropped into my socks. Carmen was all scarlet and black, and young. Much younger than my mother.

Thirteen

Carmen wasn't so keen to kiss me. She said, '*Hola*, Maria,' and gave me a bright smile. Her teeth looked strong and white between her wide scarlet lips. Then she kissed my father and murmured something secret into his ear. I couldn't catch what she said but he laughed. I knew from that moment that I would hate her.

It was not the best start to the evening and I had been looking forward to it so much! I was allowed to stand at the side of the stage out of sight, in the wings, so to speak, though there were no proper wings. After all, this was not a theatre but a dining room. People kept on clattering plates and rattling cutlery and blethering to their neighbours even after the show started. I wondered how Antonio and the others could put up with it. But, as he'd said, when he started to dance nothing else in the world mattered.

He danced brilliantly that night, especially when he did a solo, for then everyone was shut out. But when he danced with Carmen his eyes were fastened on hers. Their feet whirled and twirled and stamped and she clicked her castanets but they never lost sight of each other. I was glad when their bit ended and Sylvana got up off her chair to sing. She had a very deep and strong voice that carried into all the corners of the room without a microphone.

I joined them at the interval in the dressing room although it was a bit of a squash with five of us in there. Giorgio, the guitarist, made up the fifth.

'Did you enjoy the show?' he asked me.

I nodded.

'You must learn to dance, Maria!' said Sylvana. 'Your father will teach you!'

'I'm going to learn,' I said. And then Antonio would have no need of Carmen for a partner. He would have me. I thought Carmen looked amused when I said that I intended to learn. Her smile annoyed me.

During the next show I imagined I was up there on the dais with Antonio. I could see myself in a white dress spotted with red and a red frill round the foot. I felt the swish of the frill against my legs. I tapped one foot in time to the music.

That night I dreamt about dancing and when I awoke in the morning I asked my father when I could start having lessons.

'When we get to Seville,' he said. 'I know a very good teacher for you there.'

It then came to me that in order to train as a really good flamenco dancer I would have to *live* in Spain. But what about my mother and my friends Shona and Amy? We were to go to a school camp in the summer term which we'd been looking forward to and then after the holidays we would all go up to secondary together.

I felt mixed up again.

We packed our bag and moved on along the coast to our

next stop, just my father and I. I didn't know how Carmen was going to get there and I didn't ask. But Antonio did ask me how I'd liked her.

'She's very nice, don't you think?'

'I liked Sylvana better,' I said, looking out of my side window at the sea, which was quite choppy today.

'I hope you *will* like her,' he said. 'She is a very good friend.'

I said nothing.

It was only a short drive to Nerja. I liked it much better than the last place. We had a room in the old part of town and it felt like a *real* town where people lived and didn't just come on holiday.

We went out and strolled around the narrow streets, ending up on the Balcony of Europe. That's what the spur of land sticking out into the sea is called. It's fringed with palms and people promenade up and down, something which Antonio is fond of doing. All Spaniards are. They call it *el paseo*. It's the passing of one another that they like and seeing who's out and about.

On one side of the Balcony there are café terraces to sit out on.

'Shall we sit down?' said Antonio.

He signalled to the waiter and ordered us drinks. I sat back and half closed my eyes against the sun. It felt so good to be here with him. I was now swinging over to the idea that I *would* like to live in Spain. Perhaps I could persuade my mother to come and live here too. She wouldn't go back to Antonio, I knew she wouldn't do that. She'd said so often enough. Wild horses wouldn't drag her! But sometimes when people are worked up they say things that they don't totally mean. I know that myself! Perhaps, though, we could live *near* Antonio in Seville and Charlie and I could see him every day and I could have flamenco lessons from this fantastic teacher he's picked out for me and Shona could come and spend the summer holidays with us and who knows but in time my mother and father might get used to each other again and get back together.

'Ah, Carmen!' I heard my father say and I jumped as if someone had stuck a pin in me. I opened my eyes to see his dancing partner dancing in front of us wearing her scarlet smile. She didn't have the frills on, of course; she was dressed in black from top to toe except for a dark red carnation pinned to her hair.

'*Buenas dias!*' she cried.

Now I knew whom she reminded me of. Snow White's stepmother, the Wicked Queen! She was all got up in scarlet and black too. At least that's how I'd always thought of her. Didn't she die eating a poisoned apple?

'Do you like apples, Carmen?' I asked.

'Apples!' She laughed and looked at Antonio as if he might explain my silly question. 'Why, Maria, do you have some apples?'

'Not right now,' I said and got up. 'I think I'll go for a walk, Papa.'

'Don't go far,' he warned. 'Stay in sight.'

Not that he would have eyes to see me with! As soon as I moved away he had hold of Carmen's hand and was gazing into her eyes as if bewitched. That must be it! She'd put a spell on him. Aunt Teresa had told me that some people had the power to put spells on others. At the time I'd pooh-poohed the idea, but now I wondered if it was as off the wall as I'd thought. I must ask Aunt Teresa if she knew of any remedies for breaking spells. I wished Shona was here. Just so that I could talk to her instead of having to chat on inside my head. I knew she would giggle if I mentioned poisoned apples. 'You're awful, Maria,' she would say. Was I?

I took a turn round the Balcony, stopping at the end to gaze down at the sea boiling up around the rocks below. Leaning against the rail next to me was a family, a holiday family, consisting of a mother and a father and a boy and a girl. They seemed to be having a nice time. The girl looked about my age. They were speaking English.

I couldn't help listening in. Then I realised that they weren't actually English, but Scottish! The lilt in their voices made me feel homesick.

Could I speak to this family? I smiled at the girl and she smiled back at me. She had a friendly, freckled face. Now the mother engaged my eye and she smiled too.

'It's a long way down, isn't it?' I said.

'It certainly is!' said the mother. 'I thought you were Spanish?'

'Half. And half Scottish!'

'We're all Scottish,' said the girl with another smile.

'From Edinburgh,' said the mother.

'Edinburgh!' I said.

'You too?' said the girl.

I nodded. Could I ask for their help? Could I ask them to

contact my mother and let her know where I was? Could I tell them that my father had snatched my brother and myself from the school playground one lunchtime and was keeping us prisoner in a high white fortress? And if I did would they believe me?

I glanced back at the terrace where Antonio and Carmen sat. They weren't looking anywhere near me. I could have gone to the moon as far as they were concerned. And perhaps that was what Carmen would have liked me to do.

Fourteen

I hesitated, wondering if I could tell my story to this family from Edinburgh. And in the next instant my father called to me. 'Maria!' He was standing up and waving.

'That's my father,' I said. 'I'd better go. Have a nice holiday.'

'You, too,' chorused the family.

As I walked back to rejoin my father *and* Carmen I knew I never would have told on him. It was too much to tell. And I couldn't have brought myself to show him up so badly in front of strangers. They'd probably think he was a monster – a kidnapper! – but he wasn't really.

'Lunchtime,' said Antonio.

'I'm not hungry,' I said, eyeing Carmen, wondering if she would be coming with us. When I found she wasn't my appetite perked up.

'See you later, Antonio,' she said, kissing his cheek. '*Adios*, Maria!'

Antonio took me to a restaurant looking down over the beach. We sat under a straw umbrella and there, at the very next table, were the family from Edinburgh!

'We meet again!' said the mother.

'Hello,' I said, not as much at ease with them now.

'We're from Edinburgh,' said the father to my father.

I saw that worried Antonio.

'We just met this morning,' I said hurriedly. 'On the Balcony.'

'Do you come from Nerja?' the mother asked my father.

'No,' said my father, adding with some reluctance, 'Seville.' Normally he would be opening up his heart to strangers, telling them what a wonderful city Seville was and that they must come and visit the cathedral! But he was wary of these strangers, for obvious reasons. In a moment they might turn out to know his wife!

'You're on holiday here then, too?' said the other father.

'He's here to dance!' I said proudly.

They then had to hear all the details, where he would be performing, and when. They would come tonight to see him!

'We enjoy flamenco,' said the mother. 'But it's not always easy to find good examples.'

'My father is very good,' I said.

'She is prejudiced!' he said, smiling. He was thawing a little.

'This is Rachel,' said the mother, naming her daughter.

'I'm Maria,' I said. We both said, 'Hi!' and Rachel gave me her friendly smile again.

'Perhaps you'd like to sit with us this evening,' said Rachel's mother, 'while your father is working?'

It was difficult to refuse. We didn't accept exactly but we didn't say no either. Antonio said that was kind of them.

'I'm Helen Drummond, by the way,' said the mother, 'and this is my husband Donald and son Malcolm.'

'Antonio,' said my father, giving them a little bow.

Their fish and chips arrived so they busied themselves with

72

that. Unusually for us, Antonio and I talked quietly, as if we had secrets to hide, which of course we did.

The Drummonds finished their meal ahead of us and left saying, 'See you both tonight!'

'I want you to be careful Maria,' said Antonio.

'I know!' I said, a bit angrily. 'I know!'

'They wouldn't understand,' he said.

Not many people would, I imagined.

I went for a walk in the afternoon while he had his siesta. I couldn't sleep. He wouldn't have wanted me to go roaming about on my own but he was out for the count when I sat up and pulled on my trainers.

I wished I had some money. I hesitated. There was small change strewn across the dresser where he had dropped it when he'd emptied his trouser pockets. Could I take some? *Steal* some? It wasn't stealing exactly, was it, when it was your father's money and he wouldn't give you anything to phone your mother?

I took another look to make sure he was asleep, then I scooped up a few of the coins and slid them quietly into the pocket of my jeans. I would not use them today, I would wait until the time was ripe.

It seemed bright in the street after the dusky light of the shuttered room. A lot of the shops were closed – having their siestas too – but there were people about, holiday makers mostly. I drifted along, caught up in the stream, stopping when they did to look at the straw hats and beach balls and postcards of Nerja hanging up in front of the souvenir shops. Since coming to Spain I'd never been out on my own without someone knowing exactly where I was.

I reached the Balcony. There, sitting on a terrace drinking coffee with another woman, was Carmen. Unfortunately she saw me before I saw her.

'Maria!' she said. 'What are you doing here? Where is your father?' She didn't actually ask, 'Does he know you're out?' She didn't have to. Her raised eyebrow said it all.

'He's sleeping,' I said and walked on with my head up. I went further along the street, then I took a right turn so that I emerged into a street running parallel to the other. This enabled me to double back without re-passing Carmen. I walked briskly now, feeling guilty! I felt angry that I felt guilty. How long could we go on like this? What plans did my father have? Did he have any or was he just playing it by ear as he went along?

The door of our boarding house was not locked so I was able to return before he would know I had been out. He lay sprawled on his back still sleeping.

I was resigned to the fact that Carmen would tell him later. She was the type to klipe on anybody. But, as it happened, she didn't get the chance to tell.

Fifteen

There was a picture of the four performers on a billboard outside the hotel where they were to perform that evening. They looked very handsome and colourful in their flamenco costumes. Especially Carmen. Under each of them was written their name: Sylvana, Carmen, Antonio and Giorgio.

'Do you always perform with the same people?' I asked.

'Always!' said Antonio. 'It is necessary to know one's partners well!'

While we were standing there in front of the picture the Drummonds arrived in good time for the first performance. They were ready to sweep me up and take me off with them right then but Antonio said quickly that I was going to come backstage first, to help the ladies with their dresses. I was sure one lady wouldn't want any help from me with her dress!

The dressing room here was better than the previous one and even had a wide window looking over the car park. Giorgio was sitting in a corner softly plucking the strings of his guitar. Carmen was standing in front of a mirror pouting into it while she lipsticked her lips. Tonight she was dressed in sherbet orange and white, with a white carnation clamped to each side of her head.

'*Que bella!*' said my father, smiling at her image in the mirror.

75

How beautiful! Honestly, it would have made you sick!'

She smiled back at him. Her lips looked all glossy and sherbety in the glass. *Mirror, mirror, on the wall, who is the fairest of us all?*

Just before the first performance was due to begin I slipped back out to find the Drummonds. They had kept a place for me between Rachel and her mother and had bought me a Coke, which was nice of them. They did seem very nice.

'So which part of Edinburgh do you live in, Maria?' asked Mrs Drummond as the lights were dimming. I was relieved not to have to answer. Edinburgh might be a city with a population of half a million but in some ways it seems quite small. Wherever you go you seem to meet somebody who knows somebody you know. So says my mother, and she should know since she grew up there.

The Drummonds were very enthusiastic about the show. They clapped heartily at the end of the first half and Mr and Mrs called out 'Bravo!' and she even drummed her feet.

'Your father *is* very good,' said Mr Drummond.

'It would be nice if you and Rachel could be friends when you get back home, Maria,' said her mother. 'She's learning Spanish at school. You could give her some practice in conversation!'

Rachel had turned out to be a year older than me and was in her first year at secondary. They'd broken up for the Easter holiday. And she was at the very same school that I would be going to! This was getting too close for comfort.

There was now to be an interval.

I became aware of someone hissing at me from the side of the hall.

'There's the singer,' said Mr Drummond. 'What's her name? Sylvana? She seems to want to speak to you, Maria.'

Sylvana was signalling frantically to me.

'It must be urgent,' said Mrs Drummond.

'The Spanish, you know,' I said, 'they sometimes make a fuss . . .'

I didn't finish the sentence. I wove between the tables to reach Sylvana. As soon as I did she seized my hand.

'What's up?' I asked. 'Is Antonio all right?'

'Come along, child!' She tugged me behind her. I almost tripped over the frill of her dress until she snatched it up with her free hand.

In the dressing room the rest of the cast was in a tizzy. Especially Antonio. He was standing by the window when we came in but as soon as he saw us he sprang across the room and slammed the door behind us. You'd have thought a pack of wild dogs was snapping at our heels, baying for our blood.

'What are you going to do, Antonio?' cried Carmen.

'We'll have to go,' he said. 'There's nothing else for it. You'll have to dance without me.'

'But how *can* I?'

I hoped Carmen might be about to burst into tears and send watery streaks down her make-up.

'They will be expecting to see you, Antonio,' said Sylvana, wringing her hands. I had never seen anyone 'wring their hands' before.

'Tonight they won't! You will have to make an

announcement. Tell them I have been taken ill! Tell them I've got a fever! Anything!' He felt his brow. 'I feel fevered. This is an emergency. Come on, Maria!'

He took hold of my hand and with a quickly tossed off '*Adios*' to his partners, not even taking the time to *kiss* Carmen, he opened the door, peered out into the corridor, and yanked me after him.

We left by the back door. I had no breath left in me to ask any questions so I just allowed myself to be towed along behind him like a puppet on a string. We ran all the way back to our lodgings. We bundled our belongings into his duffel bag and he paid off the landlady, telling her that he had been called home on urgent business.

'Is Aunt Teresa ill?' I asked as we made for the car, which was parked further along the street.

'No,' he said, 'she is fine. As far as I know.'

We jumped into the car and took off with a great snarl of tyres on the gravelly road.

'Is somebody after us?' I asked, hanging on to the door strap.

'I hope not,' he said.

Somebody must be! Had he seen them from the dressing room window? The police? But the law was on his side as far as taking custody of his children was concerned. What if he had committed some other crime? What, though? He was hot-headed so I supposed he might have biffed someone in a fight if they'd challenged him. But he had no marks of a fight on him. And he'd been perfectly all right throughout the first performance, dancing with his usual vigour and concentration. Something had upset him since then.

78

I mused on other possibilities as we swung out on to the main road. He might have got into debt — he was never actually swimming in money, after all — and the debt collector might have arrived. Or a former boyfriend of Carmen's might have turned up to challenge him to a duel! If that were the case, I couldn't see him running.

'Has it anything to do with Carmen?' I asked.

'Has what?' he said, pulling out rather sharply to pass a car, which retaliated by leaning on its horn.

'Us leaving like this?'

'No, no,' he muttered. 'Don't worry about it.'

There must be *something* to worry about to make it necessary for us to take off like a couple of lunatics, scattering everything around us. I thought of the Drummonds. They would be wondering what had happened to me. They would think it very rude of me not to come back and say cheerio. I was sorry about that as I'd thought they were all right and I would have liked to have seen Rachel when I went back to Edinburgh. I didn't think she'd want to have anything to do with me now.

'Are we going back to the village tonight?' I asked. The dashboard clock said 11.35 and it was several hours' drive to the white fortress in the mountains.

'No,' said my father. 'We shall go to Cordoba and stay the night with my friend Miguel. Go to sleep and I'll wake you when we get there.'

Go to sleep! He must have been joking. There was too much to think about. I felt as wide awake as a night hawk. And the more I thought the more convinced I became that

...rried exit from the hotel must have had something to ...with my mother. Could *she* have turned up? She might have come over to Spain and been touring along the coast looking for signs of Antonio. She'd know the kind of places he'd play in. There were posters all over the place advertising him.

I didn't reveal any of my thoughts to him, nor did I ask any more questions. There was no point. He'd deny everything, anyway. And even if he didn't he wouldn't turn round and head back.

For the moment I had to hold my fire.

Sixteen

Antonio's friend Miguel didn't seem to mind being wakened in the small hours of the morning.

'Antonio!' he said, rubbing his eyes.

'This is my daughter Maria,' said my father.

'Maria!' said Miguel. 'So you have got her back! *Bueno! Bueno!* I am happy for you both. Come in! Evelina!' He shouted up the stairs for his wife.

Evelina came and she didn't complain, either. She must have been used to Miguel's friends arriving at an 'unearthly hour', as my Scottish granny would put it. I always liked the idea of an hour being unearthly, belonging to another sphere.

Evelina took me into the kitchen and gave me some warm milk and left-over *tortilla*. I felt like a pussy cat being brought in from the cold.

'We will leave the men to catch up on their gossip,' she said.

I was ready to sink into the soft feather bed she made up for me in the spare room. I must have been asleep before she closed the door behind her.

When we got up in the morning we found that both Miguel and Evelina had left for work.

A note on the kitchen table said, 'Help yourself to breakfast.

gain soon for a longer visit.'

ourselves to a breakfast of milky coffee and bread
n we were back on the road again heading north.

that we couldn't stay and see something of Cordoba
for I like new places.

Antonio was more relaxed this morning. He no longer
hunched his shoulders as he drove. I guess he reckoned we'd
left the danger well behind. After a while he began to sing. I
felt like singing, too, and did, for, after all, hadn't we left
Carmen behind! I hoped she would be angry with my father
for running off like that leaving her to dance on her own.
With a bit of luck she wouldn't want to see him again and I
wouldn't need a potion to break her spell over him. When I
remembered that we might also have left my mother behind
my singing wavered.

We drove up into the village in the middle of the afternoon.
Nobody was about. They'd all be snoozing behind their
shutters. Antonio squeezed the car into an awkward space on
the piazza and we headed up the hill.

'It's good to be back,' he said. 'There is nothing like clean
mountain air.'

'I quite like sea air,' I said.

'There are too many people down on the coast.'

One too many for you, I thought.

Aunt Teresa was just getting up from her siesta. She was
pleased to have us back.

'The boy has been restless,' she said. 'He's been missing you.'

I went through to the bedroom. Charlie was lying on the
bed sleeping with his cheek squashed against the pillow. I

82

thought he looked pale and his eyelashes glistened as if damp. Had he been crying? I felt guilty that I'd left him.

I deliberately hadn't quite shut the door. I stood close by it, listening. My father was speaking quietly but Aunt Teresa had only one voice level and that was loud.

'I told you it would be a mistake to take her!' she was saying.

Antonio murmured something.

'So she didn't see her!' said Aunt Teresa. 'That's all very well but she'll ask at the hotel surely? She's not stupid, is she, your wife? Someone will tell her you had a girl the age of Maria with you.'

Antonio murmured something else.

'Of course you will have to stay here longer,' said Aunt Teresa. 'You can't go to Seville now.'

Antonio did some more murmuring.

'If the law is on your side what do you have to worry about?' demanded Aunt Teresa in an even louder voice. Antonio hushed her and she softened it, but only slightly. 'If she tries to take them you can call the police! If you have to you have to!'

That ended their conversation. I closed the door properly and sat down on the bed. I didn't think our father would want to call the police. He'd know that might put us against him, for he wasn't any more stupid than our mother was. But they could both be unreasonable, that was the trouble.

Charlie called out in his sleep and he trembled, the way a dog does when it's having a bad dream.

'It's all right, Charlie,' I said, smoothing his blond hair back from his forehead.

He seemed to be coming to the end of his dream. His leg

jerked and his eyes fluttered a couple of times.

'Wake up, Charlie! It's me, Maria.'

'Maria!' He sat up. 'I thought you weren't coming back!'

'That was silly! You would know I would always come back.' And I wouldn't leave him again! If there were to be any more trips to the coast we would have to take him with us. But probably there wouldn't be any now. Not if our mother was around.

'Did you bring me a present?' he asked, cheering me a little. If he could think of presents he couldn't be that down in the dumps. Though he had asked in a rather small voice as if he wasn't too much bothered whether we had or not.

'We didn't have time,' I said.

'But you were away for three whole days!' His lip was trembling again.

'We had to leave the last place quickly.'

'You said.'

'I know. We'll get you a present here.'

'There are no presents in the village. I've had enough holiday. I want to go home!' He burst into tears.

Seventeen

It was out of the question to go down to the coast and look for our mother! Way out of the question. And she wouldn't be at home in Edinburgh to take any phone calls. I would just have to phone Aunt Heather. I thought about our granny but she was having a bit of trouble with her heart so I didn't think I should upset her.

'Don't worry, Charlie,' I said, 'we'll be going home soon.'

It was a big promise! He asked me to make it and I did.

'Don't say a word to Papa or Aunt Teresa!' I warned him. 'It's to be our secret.'

Next morning, I got up early, before either Charlie or Antonio. Aunt Teresa always rose at dawn. Like the birds, she said. She liked to hear their wake-up songs and see the first smudges of pink coming into the eastern sky. She would go out and stand in the street to see it since all the windows in her apartment faced west.

She was making fresh coffee when I went through to the living room. The smell made my mouth water. She ground her own beans every morning. We breakfasted together and my father slept on in the alcove untroubled by our being there.

'He sleeps like a child,' said Aunt Teresa. 'Even a clap of thunder would not disturb him.'

I asked if she'd like me to do some shopping for her. I wanted to go down to the piazza before my father went to the café for his morning coffee.

Aunt Teresa decided she needed eggs. 'And you might as well get some milk. Tell Josefa your father will pay later.'

I passed no one going down the hill.

'You are an early bird this morning!' said Josefa. 'You had a good time at the coast?'

'Very good,' I said, my eye on the phone box.

'You met your father's friends?' asked Josefa slyly.

'Yes,' I said. Did she know about Carmen?

'That's a dozen eggs.' She put them in a brown paper bag on the counter. She didn't always have boxes. 'Take care not to knock them. And a litre of milk.'

'Aunt Teresa said to tell you that my father will pay you when he comes down.' Josefa was writing in her book. The page headed 'Antonio' was full. She had to start a new one.

'He would earn some money at the coast?'

'Oh, yes,' I said, and then I wondered if he would have got any in Nerja. I didn't see how he could have done, since we'd taken off so abruptly. And he'd had to settle up with the landlady. '*Adios*, Josefa.' I escaped quickly.

I knew she would watch me from her window. She would just have to! I went into the phone box and laid the eggs very carefully on the floor.

I read the instructions for making an international call. And it was only then that I began to wonder if I would have enough money. International calls are expensive, especially in the daytime. I took the coins out of my pocket and counted them.

Two with holes in them were worth twenty-five pesetas apiece. And two little silver ones were worth five each. That made sixty pesetas. Four little coppery ones were only one peseta each. Up to sixty-four now. I dug deeper into my pocket. All was not yet lost. I still had something else down there. I pulled out two more holey coins. That made a hundred and fourteen pesetas in total. But the peseta is equal to about only half of a British one pence piece so you can see that wasn't as much money as it sounded. It wasn't enough to make a phone call to Scotland!

I dug down again into the corners of both pockets though I knew there would be nothing else there except bits of fluff. I wanted to scream at the telephone sitting there looking smug and quiet.

I glanced round and saw my father standing on the other side of the glass door looking in at me! I jumped. My left leg moved backward and I heard a soft crack. My heel must have contacted the bag of eggs.

I bent down and lifted the bag. Gooey egg yolk trickled from the brown paper bag on to my hands.

My father opened the door. I looked up at him.

'I've broken Aunt Teresa's eggs,' I said.

Eighteen

I hadn't broken them *all*. Only five. *Only* five! Aunt Teresa wouldn't be at all chuffed. She hated waste. I tried to save some of the eggs by putting the cracked sides up so that not all the yolk would run out. At the very least she might be able to make an omelette from them. But I wasn't very successful.

I was quite glad, however, of the broken eggs. For they created a diversion. My father didn't get the chance to start grilling me. He had to help with the eggs.

By the time I emerged from the phone box my hands were covered with the sticky yellow mess and I had a fair bit of it on my jeans as well as my T-shirt which had been clean that morning. With our clothes being so few we couldn't have clean ones every day.

Josefa had come across to help and get a better view – what else! She said we must come over to the shop and get sorted out. She took the soggy bag from my hands and marched us across the piazza. The old men were having a good morning!

'Wash your hands in the sink in the back room!' Josefa directed me. 'And I'll give you an old piece of rag to wipe down your jeans. Tech, tech! New clothes don't grow on trees and I have no extra eggs I can give you.' There seemed to me to be a note of joy in her voice. It's not often Josefa sounds joyful. You can't blame her I suppose when so many people owe her money.

Antonio had to wash his hands too. We shared the sink. He wasn't saying anything as yet. I kept my eyes on my hands and the mucky water.

When we went back through to the shop Josefa had put the remaining seven eggs in a clean bag, which she said Antonio should carry. But she made no direct move to give it to him, instead she produced her book of figures. Her pencil was stuck behind her ear.

'It's a while since you've settled up, Antonio.'

'Ah.' He put his hand in his pocket. 'I'm not sure how much I have on me this morning.' He brought out a few notes which he passed across to Josefa.

She counted them, and taking the pencil from her ear, marked off two or three lines of our account. 'There is still quite a lot owing.'

This was the kind of incident my mother never would get involved in. She would hate it! She earned regular money and paid her bills on time and if we couldn't afford anything we didn't have it. Money – or lack of it – can cause trouble in a relationship, my mother says. It did with her and Antonio. He says an artist can't expect to have a *regular* income. I think he's right, and that she is too.

'I shall be getting some more money soon,' said Antonio. 'From my last gig. Then, Josefa, I shall pay you every single peseta!'

None of us believed that but Josefa didn't challenge him.

She let us go, after giving me further instructions as to how to get egg yolk off jeans.

We still had Aunt Teresa to face.

'You've been a long time,' she said, when we arrived warm and puffed out from the climb. I had moved fast up the steep, cobbled road, keeping a step or two ahead of Antonio. Aunt Teresa was standing at her door. 'Charlie has been anxious. He thought you'd gone away again.'

The moment had come for me to confess my sin. Aunt Teresa moaned softly and poked in the bag with a bent finger.

'I'm sorry,' I kept saying.

'You do not know the value of money, Maria!'

On escaping I locked myself in the bathroom and set to to wash my jeans and T-shirt with a bar of soap and cold water. Then I hung them up dripping.

'Those things aren't clean enough!' Aunt Teresa snapped off the clothes pegs and taking the clothes down thrust them into the soap suds in her big tub. As her elbows pumped up and down she muttered on about my mother not having taught me properly.

'I want to speak to you, Maria,' said my father.

I followed him through to my room.

'I didn't phone anyone,' I said quickly. 'I didn't have enough money.'

'But you were trying to phone your mother, weren't you?'

'Yes, I was! Papa, we want to see her! You can't *stop* us seeing her!' Surely the Spanish court would at least allow her access so that she could visit us? And if she did I was determined that we would run off with her, the way we'd done with our father. It would be a reverse journey. Then he could come and visit us in Scotland. That would be part of the bargain that I'd make with my mother. I said, 'Charlie's unhappy!'

'It's just taking him time to settle.'

'*Settle*?' I jumped on the word. 'I thought we were only here for a holiday?'

'To start with, for a holiday.'

'And then?'

'At some point I hope to take you to Seville.'

'To *live*?'

'You like Seville, don't you?'

'Yes, but –'

'You are fond of your grandparents?'

'Yes, but –'

'And your cousins? What about your sweet cousin Rosa? Your soul mate.'

'Yes, but –' I did want to see Rosa, but I also wanted to see Shona and Amy. And my mum. Especially my mum.

'What about me, Maria?' my father asked in a sad voice. 'You like to be with me, don't you?'

'You know I do, Papa, but –'

'I love you and little Charlie.' He raised his arms in a despairing gesture before letting them flop. Then he cried, 'Maria, I cannot give you up!'

Nineteen

I burst into tears and my father opened his arms to me. He hugged me tight. He cried, too. We cried together.

When we'd dried our eyes and I'd sniffled a bit I asked, 'What are we going to do?'

'I cannot give you up, Maria,' he said again. 'I just *cannot*! Those two years when I didn't see you nearly killed me. I thought of you every day.'

And I'd thought of him every day.

'Remember,' he said, 'that your mother stopped me from seeing you! She told me lies to keep us apart.'

You could say that she deserved what was happening to her now, because of what she'd done, but I didn't want to say it. I didn't know what to say any more, or to do. I felt as if a sharp little spike was piercing my heart. I kept rubbing the left side of my chest but it wouldn't go away. As far as I knew children of my age didn't have heart attacks. I felt, though, as if my heart was being attacked.

Antonio made a drink for us by squeezing fresh oranges. We took our glasses out on the balcony. For the time being we had run out of words. We sat quietly looking out at the incredible mountain view. It looked so mysterious and so peaceful, and I felt so sad. Beside me, Antonio sighed.

Our silence was broken by the arrival of Donatila, the neighbour who had the telephone. She came into the living room calling, 'Antonio! Telephone!'

He went off straight away while Donatila lingered to study our view. 'It fills you with awe, doesn't it, child? We are so little and the mountains are so vast and so eternal. They will still be there when you and I have turned to dust, Maria.'

I didn't want to do that yet, turn to dust, but she, like Aunt Teresa, was very old and perhaps did not mind the idea so much. Aunt Teresa said that God was out there, among the mountains. I sent out a little prayer to him, asking for help.

'Was the phone call from a woman?' I asked.

My question caught Donatila off guard. 'Why, yes. His friend Carmen.'

That roused me from my mood of melancholy, though I could still feel the spike in my heart.

When my father returned I asked him, 'What did Carmen want?'

'To know if we got back safely.' He sat down beside me again. 'You don't seem to like her, Maria? Every time you say her name I hear the barb in your voice. That saddens me.'

'She doesn't like me, either!'

'How can you say that!'

'Because she gives me cold looks. She is jealous of me. *She* would like me to go back to Scotland.'

'I'm sure that is not true! She is a very kind lady.'

They say that love can be blind. How did he not see that she had a tongue that dripped with acid and a heart as black as the blackest night?

93

'You used to love Mummy,' I said.

'And she used to love me.'

'Can't you love one another again?' I cried. If they had once in the past why not again in the future?

'The past is past, Maria. It cannot easily be found again.'

'If you *tried*.'

'Do you think your mother would want to?'

'She wouldn't want to give up her job.' I knew that didn't answer his question. I said, 'She's in Spain, isn't she? That was why we left Nerja in such a hurry, wasn't it?'

'Yes.' He said it openly as if he was no longer going to tell me any lies.

'How did you know she was there?' I asked.

'I looked out of the dressing room window and there she was getting out of a car in the car park!'

'She must have seen one of your posters.'

'That's possible.'

'Why shouldn't we get in touch with her now and tell her where we are?'

'She would come, and there would be trouble. I don't want you children to be caught up in a tug of war.'

'It needn't be like that!'

'No? She would try to take you away, yet she would have no right to.'

'Under Spanish law!'

'This is Spain!'

'You don't have to tell me!'

'If she tried to take you without permission she could be arrested. For contempt of court.' He took my hand. 'Maria, once things have settled down you can see her and spend holidays with her. As long as she would promise to return you to Spain afterwards.'

I couldn't imagine our mother agreeing to that!

Twenty

I tired myself out thinking about it. When I was putting Charlie to bed that night he asked me again, 'We are going home soon, aren't we?'

'Yes, yes. But not *straight* away.'

'You promised!'

'You have to be patient, Charlie. You have got to give me time.'

Time to do what? I had to talk to somebody but I didn't know whom or how. That night I dreamt about being trapped in an alley with high white walls on either side and at each end. I was running frantically up and down batting my hands against the stone. When I awoke the palms of my hands were sore.

Antonio took both Charlie and me down to the café in the morning. I felt he had decided not to let us out of his sight. We were sitting sunning ourselves when who should come up to the shop but Paula and her father. He was driving a pick-up truck with onions and tomatoes heaped in the back. He'd brought them to sell to Josefa.

Paula and I kind of nodded at one another. She helped her father carry in the vegetables. Her arms looked brown and thin but wiry.

'Hey, Maria!' Josefa signalled to me from her doorstep.

I went over to her.

'Paula would like you to go home with them. She can show you the farm.' And stop me from sitting about doing nothing! That was probably what Josefa was thinking. She'd told me the other day that I didn't have enough to do, I should be going to school.

The schools had broken up for the Easter holidays. The day after tomorrow would be Good Friday. The villagers had been decorating a float, with a statue of Christ set in the middle, surrounded by masses of red and white flowers. The men were to carry it up to the church from the bottom of the hill, to signify Jesus carrying the cross. It would take eight strong men to carry the heavy float on their shoulders. Antonio was to be one of them.

Paula stood with her head half bowed. I doubted if she'd have said anything about wanting to take me home. If I knew Josefa she would have suggested it herself. But it didn't seem a bad idea to me. I was feeling restless and it would be good to get out of the village for a while. My father was consulted. He spoke to Paula's father, and it was agreed I should go. Paula's father said he would bring me back to the piazza at six o'clock, and Antonio would meet me.

Paula and I squashed on to the front seat of the pick-up together and I held on to the open window ledge. We rolled down the hill to the foot of the village and then bumped the three further kilometres over a rutted track.

Their farm was a rather ramshackle affair though there were neat polythene sheets covering the rows of tomatoes and cucumbers. The polythene brought the vegetables on more quickly, Paula's father explained.

There hadn't been any rain for a while so the red earth was dry. Chickens skittered about pecking in the dust and a cow chomped on a patch of grass, while half a dozen goats were penned into a small area of their own. If they weren't fenced in they would eat everything in sight! said Paula's father. The farmhouse looked as if it could be doing with some running repairs but they didn't seem to spend much time inside it, not even Paula's mother.

She gave us soup for lunch and hunks of bread. We ate inside the dark kitchen. I couldn't see what was in the soup but it tasted good. They didn't speak much while they ate though when they had finished they did ask me a few of the questions I had come to expect. How did I like Spain? Was it always cold in Scotland? Did it rain all the time?

After lunch Paula and I went out to milk the goats. I'd never milked a goat before but I was willing to give it a try. She showed me how to go about it. Goats aren't the easiest of animals to get on with, so I was to find out. Mine was very frisky and kept kicking me in the shins until I longed to kick it back and when I did manage to squeeze a trickle of milk from its teat she gave the bucket a swipe with her hoof and my hard-won milk went swooshing all over my lower legs. The jeans would need washing again!

Paula and I couldn't help laughing, though. I started, and she joined in. We sat on the ground and laughed until tears were running down our faces. I don't suppose it was all that funny but we'd needed something to break the ice for us. We stopped just before we got too hysterical. My stomach ached. But at least it was from laughing and not crying.

After that Paula and I got on really well together. She wasn't as shy as she'd seemed. I told her all about my school and she told me about hers. A bus collected her in the mornings and took her to the school twenty kilometres away. It went all round the area picking up children, just the way buses did in the rural areas of Scotland.

'But you won't be coming to our school, will you?' she said. 'I wish you were! You will be going to school in Seville.'

So she knew that! And also that our father had had to go to court to get custody of us.

'Paula,' I said, 'everything is in a mess. My brother wants to go home. He is only six. He misses our mother. But our father doesn't want to give us up.'

'And you? What do you want?'

'I want my mother and my father. But I can't have both, not all of the time.'

'So what then?'

'I don't know.'

'My mother says she is sorry for your mother,' said Paula. 'She can imagine what she feels.'

'She can?' This gave me a small feeling of hope. I drew a circle in the red earth with a stick. 'Paula, would you help me?' I asked.

Twenty-one

I told her the whole story.

'So you see, I have to let my mother know where we are!'

'But you're not sure where she is! She might not be in Nerja any longer.'

'If I could phone my Aunt Heather she would get in touch with her.' I reckoned that my mother would be bound to keep in touch with her sister in case news of us reached Edinburgh.

I then told Paula what my problem was. I didn't have enough money to make the phone call!

'It's not much,' I added apologetically.

'Is that *all*? I can easily lend it to you. *Give* it to you.'

'I'll pay you back. When I can.'

'You don't have to. It's nothing much! Let's go inside.'

Her mother was outside hoeing a patch of pimentos so we had the house to ourselves. There was a telephone on the dresser. My hand itched to lift the receiver. Paula said she didn't think she could let me use the phone, not without asking her mother. And she thought her mother, though she might be sympathetic, wouldn't want to go against my father's wishes.

'I guess not,' I agreed sadly.

I followed Paula into her white bedroom. A vivid orange and blue spread glowed on her bed and posters of pop singers and flamenco dancers brightened her walls. She pulled a tin from under her bed. She was saving up for a CD player. She loved music. There didn't seem to be many Spaniards who didn't.

She gave me five hundred pesetas.

'Are you sure?' I asked.

'Very sure! Will it be enough?'

'Oh yes! I'm just going to make a quick call.'

The next thing to resolve was how to make the call before my father came to meet me.

'You must leave early,' said Paula. 'I'll ask my father to take you at half past five. Then you'll be back in the village before your father expects you.'

There was always the chance that he would be sitting outside the café! But that I would have to risk.

Paula told her father that I was worried about my brother and wanted to go home early. He didn't question it. Paula rode with me again. There was no sign of Antonio's car at the foot of the village when we arrived there, or in the piazza. He might have gone off somewhere, thinking I was safely out of the way!

Paula's father asked if I would be all right. 'Can you go the rest of the way on your own?'

'Oh, yes, thank you. Thank you very much!'

'See you on Good Friday!' said Paula. She was coming up to the village for the celebrations. 'Good luck!' she added in a whisper.

I waited until the truck had its nose pointing downhill, then I went quickly to the phone box. I couldn't believe it! There was someone in there already, a woman whom I had passed a few times in the street but didn't know. She would know me, though. Everyone did.

She had her back to the piazza and she was chatting twenty to the dozen. I listened to the rise and fall of her voice and did a little circle round the box. She saw me but she didn't stop talking.

There were four old men in their usual seats. The heads of three drooped as they slept but the fourth was wide awake, leaning on his stick and missing nothing. I felt like sticking out my tongue at him. I took a few steps away from the booth as if I had no intention of going in. Then I heard '*Adios*' coming from its interior and raced back. The woman was coming out. She held the door open for me and I said '*Gracias*!' and slid inside.

My fingers were fumbly as I put in the coins. I almost dropped one, and caught it on the rebound. I knew the international code for the United Kingdom by heart. As I dialled I watched where the street coming up joined the piazza. The phone was ringing in Aunt Heather's house in Edinburgh. I imagined my aunt coming from the kitchen wiping her hands on a towel as she went to answer it. My heart was pumping madly. The phone went on ringing. And ringing. And ringing.

'Answer it!' I cried.

She didn't. She couldn't be at home. And she didn't have an answering machine. She said she hated the damned things, they were just a nuisance, and when you came in it cost you a fortune returning the calls.

I put down the receiver. I would just have to phone my granny and risk upsetting her.

I dialled her number. I heard the ringing tone begin. I waited. It could take her a while to get to the phone. She was a bit slow on her feet since she'd had her bad turn. The phone went on ringing. And ringing. Oh *no*! I didn't know whether to cry or kick the wall. I was about to give up when I heard a click at the other end.

'Hello,' she said, her voice as clear as if she were in the next room, 'this is Mary MacKenzie speaking.'

'Granny!' I gulped.

'Maria!' she cried. 'Is that you, love?'

'I thought you were out!'

'I was in the loo! Are you all right?'

'Yes.'

'You don't sound all right.'

I was snivelling. Tears were running down my nose. 'It's just –' I couldn't go on. It was just an awful lot of things.

'Where are you?' she asked.

I told her just as my father wrenched open the door.

Twenty-two

'I trusted you, Maria,' he said sadly, which made me feel worse than if he'd shouted at me. To make myself feel better I shouted back at him.

'Why should I trust you? You told us a lie! You said you were only taking us for a holiday when you'd no intention of giving us back!'

'You know why I did it!' His anger was rising now.

I shrank back against the wall of the booth. I wasn't afraid he would hit me, nothing like that. It was more a feeling of wanting to shrivel up and disappear.

He was holding the door wide open but I didn't want to come out. 'Come out of there, Maria!' he demanded. 'You can't stay here for the rest of the day. You're not a baby.'

I flounced out and stamped off up the hill ahead of him. He made no attempt to catch me up. He walked a couple of paces behind.

When I reached Aunt Teresa's I went straight into my bedroom and slammed the door. I sat on the bed.

He came in and closed the door.

'Who did you speak to?' he asked.

'Granny,' I said, taking delight in telling him. 'Granny MacKenzie.'

'Did you tell her where you were?'

'No,' I said, crossing my fingers behind my back to cancel out the lie. 'I didn't have time.'

'I want you to pack your clothes, Maria. And Charlie's. We're leaving first thing in the morning.'

'You can if you want,' I said. 'I'm not going anywhere.' I folded my arms across my chest. I'd had enough of charging round the country from one place to the other. So it had seemed exciting to begin with, but no longer. I wouldn't go, no matter what he said. He'd have to carry me kicking and screaming down the hill, with Charlie crying his head off trailing behind us. Did he want to do that, with all the village turned out to watch?

'Listen,' he said, pulling up a chair, changing his tune.

'I don't want to listen.'

'We'll go to Seville. You've been saying you want to see your grandmother and your cousins. Your mother can come and see you there. I promise you she can.'

'I want her to come here. And when she does we're going to go home with her, Charlie and me. You can get the policeman up if you want. I'll scratch his eyes out.'

'You're talking like a baby!'

'I know! And normally everyone says I'm so grown up for my age!'

'Maria, are you really going to leave me?' he cried.

I felt myself wobble. 'I don't want to,' I muttered. 'But I want to go home. And so does Charlie.'

'Why *not* come to Seville? Everything can be sorted out more easily there.'

'That's where the stupid court is, is that what you mean?'

'I am your father and your legal guardian.'

'Are you going to *drag* us down the hill?' I asked. 'By the hair?'

He got up and left the room. Charlie came through a moment or two later.

'What's wrong?' he cried.

'Nothing. But I think we'll be going home fairly soon.'

Though even as I said it I didn't feel at all confident that we would be. Our mother might come but she might not be able to leave the country with us. We might be stopped at the airport. We might have to drive up to the French border and cross on foot. I had a vision of us walking in the pitch black of night over a pass in the Pyrenees. I had read a book once about children in the Second World War doing just that with some resistance fighters. The idea had appealed to me at the time.

In bed that night I felt restless. It was a warm night. I kept fidgeting and scratching my legs. I got up and went to the open window. I leaned out looking at the stars in the black velvety sky and once my eyes had adjusted I could make out the faint line of the mountains. Not the Pyrenees of course. They were way up north. It would be a long drive and there was the problem of how we would get away from the village to begin with.

Dots of light sparkled in the valley below. I wondered if one of them might be the lights of my mother's car. Could she have come this far yet? I guessed she could, or at least be arriving within the next few hours. It would depend on how quickly our granny had been able to contact her.

106

A new worry now gripped me. Our mother, when she came to the village, would not know *exactly* where we were. She could walk up and down the jumble of streets and alleyways until she was blue in the face but she wouldn't see us. I knew our father wouldn't allow us to go out and Aunt Teresa's flat was at the back with no windows on to the street. Even if she called our names we wouldn't hear her. The walls were thick.

She could ask at the shop or the café, but they might not tell her. It was more than possible. Antonio would only have to ask. He had probably already asked. He had gone out briefly to make a phone call at Donatila's while we were eating. 'My wife is going to come and try to steal the children from me,' he could have told them. The word would have spread quickly round the village. They would all be on his side.

Our mother might come up to the village and not find us and go away.

Twenty-three

I pulled on jeans, a T-shirt, and trainers, and at the last moment reached for my anorak. It might be cold out there. Charlie was fast asleep, snoring very gently on his back. I opened the door and listened. I could hear the steady, deep breathing of my father coming from the living room. There was no sound at all from Aunt Teresa's room.

I tiptoed along the passage. My hand found the door knob. The door was locked, as I'd expected. But the key was usually kept in the lock, in case of fire, so that it could be unlocked quickly. Tonight, the key was not there. My father seemed determined to keep us prisoner!

Then I thought of the toilet window. It opened on to the passage, the only window that did. I went in and locked the door.

The window was set half way up the wall and quite small but I thought I could just squeeze through. I climbed on to the loo seat and unsnibbed the window. It swung inward. I grasped the sill and pulled myself up until my knees rested on it. I would have to wriggle out arms first. Could I do it? Would I fall on my head?

I paused when I'd got my head and shoulders out. Luckily a light was left burning all night in the passage so that I could see where I was going. Right underneath me was a planter filled with geraniums. I might have to mangle one or two but I couldn't help that.

I let myself slither down the wall and then I let go. My arms and shoulders jarred as they hit the planter but I rolled over quickly and jumped to my feet. I stuffed a couple of flowers back into the soil and smoothed it over.

The wrought-iron gate was locked, but I knew where the key was kept. I reached up and took it from its hook on the wall. A minute later I was on the other side of the gate, in the street, free!

I ran lightly, on the soles of my feet, keeping close to the walls, taking care not to slip on the cobbles. The village was fast asleep. Not even a dog was barking.

A cat ran in front of me, giving me a fright. It disappeared into the shadows of an alley with a sweep of its long black tail. At least it was a black cat! It was meant to be lucky when a black cat crossed your path. I could do with some luck.

When I got to the piazza I stopped to catch my breath. It felt strange to be standing here, alone, in the dead of night, with the few streetlamps casting pools of light and shadow, and the shop and café shuttered, and nobody sitting on the benches. I thought I saw someone move beside one of the parked cars. Swiftly I ducked behind another and crouched down on my hunkers, with one hand touching the ground to steady myself. I was in need of steadying. I waited, and watched. My mouth was dry and I felt as if something was crawling up the back of my neck. After a few minutes I decided I must have been mistaken. There seemed to be nobody there.

But I felt afraid now, for the first time since jumping out of Aunt Teresa's toilet window. I stayed where I was, with the car acting as a shield to protect me. Every little noise sounded loud in my ears. I froze at the slightest rustle, which turned out to be only a puff of wind, a few dry leaves drifting in the gutter, a grey cat padding stealthily across the piazza. It was Josefa's cat. She had a white star on her forehead though I couldn't see the star now. Looking up I saw that the stars were still there winking above me.

The church clock began to strike. Once, twice, three times. Three o'clock! The chiming seemed to unblock my limbs, and I stood up. I licked my lips to take some of their dryness away, swallowed, and crossed the piazza.

I took the street leading down to the entrance of the village. There was a seat at the bottom where old men liked to sit and watch for approaching traffic. I squatted in a corner of it, hugging my knees to my chest. I was glad of my anorak for the air was cool. Perhaps it was as well that it was for it would help me to stay awake. I told myself that I must *not* go to sleep. If I did I might miss my mother.

A dog barked somewhere down in the valley. It might be one of Paula's father's dogs. I thought of Paula fast asleep under the woven coloured bedspread in her white room. I must ask my mother if she could come and visit us in Edinburgh.

After the dog stopped barking it was very quiet. I yawned. I felt my eyelids sinking and with an effort I forced them apart. I yawned again. I gave up thinking. I couldn't think any more. I fell asleep.

Twenty-four

'Maria!' I was awakened by someone saying my name in my ear and shaking my shoulder. '*Maria*! said the voice again, a very familiar voice. I leapt up.

There in front of me stood my mother!

'Mum!' I yelled and hurled myself at her. We hugged and I felt tears spurting from my eyes. She was crying, too.

'Oh, Maria!' she said. 'I've missed you!'

I couldn't speak. My throat felt swollen.

'What were you doing here?' she asked. 'Sleeping?'

'Waiting for you!' I clung to her, never wanting to let her go. She stroked my hair.

'Where's Charlie?'

'At Aunt Teresa's.'

'And your father?' Her voice croaked a bit.

'He's there too.'

'We'd better go up and see them then, hadn't we?'

She left her hired car at the bottom of the village and we walked up together. I took her hand. At my age I don't usually go out holding her hand, I leave that to Charlie, who likes to swing on the end of her arm. But this morning I needed to hold on.

It was full daylight by now. Josefa was opening up the shop as we reached the piazza.

111

'*Buenas dias*, Josefa,' I said. 'This is my mother.'

'*Buenas dias*,' said Josefa, her eyes popping.

On the way up the hill I told my mother something of what had been happening to us, not in detail, of course. It would have taken far too long to do that.

'I could kill your father for putting you through all that!' she declared.

'Don't, Mum,' I pleaded.

'Do you realise what I've been through too! When your Aunt Heather rang me in Sheffield to tell me your father had snatched you from the school playground I nearly went crazy.'

'I know, Mum.' I squeezed her hand.

'I went to London and flew to Seville that same day. I haven't had a minute's peace since.'

'I wanted to phone but I didn't have any money.'

'I imagine that damned father of yours saw to it you didn't get your hands on any either!'

She was getting steamed up. I couldn't blame her, but it wasn't going to help matters when we got to Aunt Teresa's.

'You realise, don't you, that your father has the legal right to keep you here?'

'Yes,' I said. We were nearly there.

'If he won't be reasonable, and I have no reason to think that he will be, I'm just going to have to snatch the two of you back the way he did. We'll have to wait for an opportunity and go for it.'

'But, Mum, he could set the police on us.'

'Just let him try!'

We were at Aunt Teresa's door. The next bit was going to be

112

terrible, I felt sure, but there could be no holding back now.

I pushed the wrought-iron gate and it swung inward. The key was still in the other side of the lock, where I'd left it. So no one had been out yet.

I had to ring the bell at the inner door. It was opened almost immediately by my father. His hair was tousled, and he was barefoot and in pyjamas.

'Maria! Where have you been?' Then he noticed my mother.

'*Buenas dias*, Antonio,' she said. 'Can we come in? I think we have some business to discuss.'

Charlie, who must have heard her voice, came rushing down the hall almost knocking Antonio over. Antonio stepped aside and Charlie hurled himself at our mother.

'Charlie, Charlie,' she said, holding his head and rocking him to and fro. 'You've no idea how much I've missed you.'

She'd missed me too, she'd told me so, but I felt a little pang of jealousy as I watched her cuddle Charlie. He was her baby. And I was her big girl. Sometimes I didn't feel too big. But big or small, I was my father's favourite.

Aunt Teresa now joined us.

'Come inside! We don't want the whole world to know our family affairs!'

'They already do,' I said.

We went into the living room and Aunt Teresa made fresh coffee and cut some bread, but none of us had any appetite. My father disappeared briefly to put on jeans and a T-shirt. Charlie sat on our mother's knee with his arm round her neck.

'We have to talk about this calmly and rationally, Antonio,' said our mother.

'I am calm,' he said, 'and rational.' He didn't look too calm to me, though our mother seemed to be. I doubted if it would last.

'I am going to take the children back to Scotland,' she said. 'That is their home now.'

'They were born in Spain,' he said. 'They are Spanish citizens. They have lived here longer than in Scotland. The court says —'

'I know what the court says!' cried my mother, losing her cool first. 'And it means nothing to me. Ask the children where they want to live!'

'I want to go home,' said Charlie.

'Maria?' she turned to me.

'I don't know,' I said miserably.

'She wants to stay with me,' said my father triumphantly. 'You do, don't you, Maria?'

'I don't know,' I said again.

'Perhaps we have to compromise,' said my father to my mother. 'Charlie can go with you and Maria can stay with me.'

'I can't give up Maria!' said my mother.

'Maria, what do you say?' asked my father.

'I don't know.' I was like a parrot!

'I won't agree to it, Antonio,' said my mother. 'No way!'

'You are not in the best position to agree or disagree,' said my father, his eyes sparking. 'You'd better remember that!'

'What kind of father do you think you are, anyway?'

demanded my mother. 'Taking the children away like that, frightening the wits out of them, and me, and their teachers at school, and their friends, and my mother, who has just about had another heart attack!'

'And what kind of mother do you think you are?' demanded our father, 'not letting me see my children for two years and telling me lies! Can you blame me for going to court? They *are* my children, too! And I love them!'

'You have a funny way of showing it!'

'Stop it!' I cried. 'Stop it, both of you.'

I ran from the room into the bedroom and launched myself face downward on the bed. At that moment I hated them both.

Twenty-five

It was Aunt Teresa who came to see me. She sat on the bed beside me and stroked my hair. Her fingers were amazingly gentle.

'Sometimes grown-up people can behave very badly,' she said. 'And be very stupid.'

'They're both stupid!' I sat up.

'Neither wants to give you up, that is the trouble.'

'But what are we going to do?' I cried. My head ached from thinking about it. I could see that my hopes of my parents getting together again had been quite wild.

'Let us think, Maria. You and me.'

We thought, and by the time we'd finished thinking we had a plan to propose to my parents.

'If they don't agree they are even stupider than I thought!' said Aunt Teresa.

We went back to the living room together. My mother was sitting on one side of the room clutching Charlie, my father on the other side. Neither was speaking. I wondered if Aunt Teresa had told them to sit there and not say another word until she came back!

'Maria has something to put to you,' she said.

This was what I proposed: that Charlie and I should live in

Scotland in term-time with our mother and come over to Spain for every holiday. Also, that Antonio should tell the court that this is what he agreed so that it would all be legal. And there was to be no more snatching on either side!

'Do you mean go to Spain for the *whole* of every holiday?' asked my mother. 'That's far too much! Charlie wouldn't want to be away from me for so long. And what about Christmas?'

I hadn't thought about Christmas. 'We could spend it with Papa, and New Year with you,' I said.

'I've never had a Christmas apart from you!'

'But I have,' said our father.

'So, Antonio,' said Aunt Teresa, after a pause, 'do you agree?'

'Yes,' he said, 'I agree. The children have had enough.'

'Oh, have they indeed?' Our mother rounded on him. 'You started it all, taking them away –'

'*I* started it?' he demanded.

'Stop!' I cried.

'Yes, stop!' said Aunt Teresa in a fierce voice. 'You are like children yourselves! Maria is more grown-up than you are.'

They stopped. My mother sighed. 'I'm sorry,' she said, looking at me. 'Neither of us has been very fair to you.'

'That's all right,' I mumbled.

'We must have a truce, Fiona,' said Antonio. 'The other way is no good.'

She nodded.

'Is it agreed then?' asked Aunt Teresa. 'I have your word, both of you?'

They gave her their word.

'I am witness to this,' she said.

The next day was Good Friday.

'Nobody is allowed to quarrel on Good Friday,' said Aunt Teresa.

Our mother shared Charlie's bed that night. There was no hotel in the village, or B&B.

We got up in the morning and had breakfast all together and my mother and father were on their best behaviour and passed the butter and jam to one another, saying 'Please' and 'Thank you' with perfect politeness. Then Antonio had to go off to join the men who were carrying the Easter float.

We put on the best clothes we had, which were not proper 'best clothes', but all we had, and our mother had to wear the jeans and shirt she'd worn to drive up here. Aunt Teresa put on her best black silk and a black straw hat and took our mother's arm going down the hill.

We stood in the piazza with the other villagers and waited for the float to come up the hill. Paula was there with her mother and father and I introduced them to our mother. Everybody was having a good look at her and wondering what was going on.

The float arrived. Antonio was one of the two men at the front. He looked very strong as he shouldered his burden. We went into the church, which was filled with the smell of Easter lilies.

After the mass we went down the hill to collect Antonio's car. We piled in and drove to a restaurant a few kilometres away. We had a really jolly lunch and nobody would have known that our mother and father were not the best of friends.

They chatted and laughed, like anybody else's mother and father.

We flew home the next day, Charlie and my mother and I. I drove down to Malaga with my father and Charlie went in the car with our mother. I cried when I said goodbye to my father at the airport. Tears spilled from me in every direction, I just couldn't stop them.

'It's all right, Maria,' he said. 'You'll be back in the summer.'

And we were. We stayed with Aunt Teresa for a couple of weeks and I saw Paula every day and we made plans for her to come over to Edinburgh next year. And then we went down to Seville to see the rest of our family and my father started to teach me to dance. We danced together in the courtyard of his house and my grandparents and cousins came to watch us and they all said I was going to be good, like my father!

I saw Carmen only twice and she seemed to be doing her best to be nice to me. I have to give her that. But I still didn't like her very much.

'It takes time to like people,' said Antonio.

At the end of our holiday, he drove us to the airport.

I felt down in the dumps at leaving him. I hate saying goodbyes.

'Cheer up, love!' said Antonio. 'Think of it this way – you are having the best of both worlds.'

Well, maybe not *quite* the best, for to do that we'd have had to have had two lives going at the same time, one to allow us to be in Scotland all year round, and the other in Spain.

He put us in the charge of the flight attendant who would see us on to the plane.

'See you at Christmas!' he said.

We waved until we turned a corner and lost sight of him.

On the plane, Charlie said, 'Mummy will be there, won't she?'

'Of course.'

The plane banked, and I saw the familiar land with its red earth and olive green shrubs and white houses tilt beneath us, and then we soared away up into the brightness of the sky.